The
Whispering
Trees

Charles E. Cravey

In His Steps Publishing

All scripture is from the King James Version of the Holy Bible.

ISBN: 978-1-58535-042-1 (Print)

ISBN: 978-1-58535-043-8 (EPUB)

ISBN: 978-1-58535-044-5 (KINDLE)

Library of Congress Catalog Number: 2025902086

Cravey, Charles E. *The Whispering Trees.*

Statesboro, Georgia: In His Steps Publishing, 2025. 252 pages.

ISBN: 978-1-58535-100-8. LCCN: 2025902086.

Cover art by Book Brush.

Contents

Foreword

Rev. Dr. Charles Cravey invited me to read *The Whispering Trees* and then write a foreword if I enjoyed it. That you are now reading this testifies to my enjoyment! I eagerly accepted his invitation and felt honored to read his work. Charles is a retired pastor in my congregation and a man of many talents! I am grateful for his support and that of his wife, Renee.

Let me begin by saying I am a novice hiker and have not yet attempted the Appalachian Trail. However, as I read this book, I not only enjoyed seeing the trail through the eyes of the characters, but I learned more about its history. Part of its allure is its mystery and the legends surrounding it. The Trail is an apt metaphor for life, where, for all the advances human civilization has made, there are still things that we cannot explain.

A few years ago, I had the privilege of spending a week

at the Grand Canyon in Arizona. Apart from its breath-taking beauty and majesty, I was also acutely aware of the dangers it presented. To venture carelessly into the canyon is to invite potential injury or even death. Walk too close to the edge, and the results can be disastrous. It is beautiful, yet simultaneously dangerous. One must respect its beauty at all costs.

It is not unlike the Appalachian Trail: captivating yet keeping mystery and even danger. If anything, the college students hikers in this book learn this is true. Even when one is prepared to the best of one's ability, the trail presents challenges, and disaster can strike without warning. Life is the same way: it is good and necessary for us to be prepared, but sometimes there are unexpected twists and turns that no amount of preparation can avoid. As human beings, we are minor compared to God's great, big world. However, the message of togetherness within this wide world resonates in this book. The beauty of human relationships in our shared triumphs and challenges makes the journey on the Trail—and through life—worthwhile. I recommend the reading of this book to anyone who enjoys an exceptional adventure and a bit of mystery. Have your Kleenex ready just in case and enjoy!

Rev. Lauren West

Associate Pastor

Statesboro First United Methodist Church

Prologue

Death is imminent. Amid the vastness of life's journey, it's the silent weaver, threading doubt, fear, and frayed edges into a tapestry of existence. Uncertainty whispers through the wind, carried across valleys and mountaintops, while death listens, ever patient. In the wild heart of the Appalachian Trail, death grants life its precious significance.

Tomorrow looms like a fragile vessel on stormy seas, its cargo unknown. The trail, with its challenges and mysteries, promises nothing. Each footstep vanishes as quickly as it appears, and with each passing tide, death's waves wash away the path.

As the twilight of their journey nears, our hikers dance in the shadows of an unseen sun, the uncertainty of their constant partner, and death their last waltz.

Where does one turn when the wilderness sings its haunting lullaby, when faced with the worst day alone and lost on the trail? How does tragedy become the last rational encounter before the darkness?

It all started so innocently. Four friends, seeking the adventure of a lifetime. In youth, there's nothing more captivating than the present moment, the thrill of the unknown, and the call of nature. "The journey matters more than the destination," they believed, even without knowing the destination might be closer than they thought.

Wrapped in the innocence of unawareness, they set off. Fate wove its intricate patterns, and life danced before them. The sun, a golden witness, painted the sky with hues of promise. Four souls, standing in the quiet dawn, dew still clinging to the petals, prepared to collide on the Appalachian Trail, their paths intersecting like celestial stars.

Innocence veiled their eyes. They laughed, whispered secrets, traced constellations on each other's skin. The world spun on its axis, pulling them along in its gravity. Whispers carried promises, but innocence unraveled with the rising sun.

Life, the master of metamorphosis, cracked their cocoon of naivety, revealing wings yearning for flight. Innocence gave way to knowledge, and the sun cast shadows once more. Betrayal and regret seeped into their hearts, doubt tasting like salt on parted lips. Innocence lost.

So it goes, the tale of us all—innocence, like morning mist, dissipates under the weight of experience. In those fleeting moments, where hearts collide and laughter echoes, we find our truest selves.

It all started so innocently, yet nothing was ever the same.

1

Danger on Black Mountain

A s the early spring sun filtered through the trees of
the Appalachian Trail, casting dappled shadows on
the forest floor, the group's laughter echoed through the
dense foliage. They had been hiking for hours, their backpacks filled with supplies and their spirits high. The air was
crisp and invigorating, and the beauty of nature surrounding them seemed to energize their steps.

Leading the group was Brian, a young man with an
insatiable thirst for adventure. He was so excited that his
fellow hikers couldn't help but get caught up in his enthusiasm. Instead of sticking to the main white trail, Brian
ventured onto a blue side trail. White and blue markers
mark the Appalachian Trail from beginning to end. The
white markers show the main course, carefully mapped
out by the Appalachian Trail council. Backpackers con-
sidered this trail the safest option, with better viewpoints
and notable sights to enjoy.

The blue trails were for the more daring and risk-taking adventurers. These trails were more challenging, with potential dangers such as washed-out sections or boulders obstructing the path. Choosing to follow a blue trail required a willingness to take risks and a sense of adventure. Thankfully, Jake, an experienced hiker in the group, reassured Brian that this blue trail was worth the effort. Although tougher, it promised breathtaking views and a chance to stand on a rocky ledge near the summit of Black Mountain, overlooking a vast valley below. If one strained their eyes, they could even glimpse the distant city of Dahlonega.

"Brian let's opt for the blue trail up ahead," Jake suggested. "I think you'll find it well worth the effort."

"Will do, Boss!" Brian chuckled; his excitement was palpable. "Your wish is my command. Come on, team, let's go adventuring!"

While Brian was giddy with anticipation, not everyone in the group shared the same level of enthusiasm. Mia and Roz, although intrigued, were skeptical about taking a trail like this. They were unsure of what challenges lay ahead and what surprises awaited them. However, being followers rather than leaders, they trusted in the judgment of their more experienced companions and will obey their commands.

As they continued along the trail, they quickly realized that their decision to venture onto the blue trail had its consequences. The path was muddy, with patches of standing water from the recent rainstorm. Puddles formed along the trail, making their progress slower and more treacherous. Despite the challenging conditions, the group pressed on, their determination unwavering.

With every step, they grew closer to the summit of Black Mountain, their anticipation building. The promise of stunning vistas and the thrill of exploring the unknown propelled them forward. Little did they know, this blue trail would test not only their physical endurance but also their resilience and teamwork.

Suddenly, a loose patch of gravel betrayed Brian, causing him to lose his footing near the cliff's edge. Time seemed to slow as his arms flailed to regain balance, but gravity's pull was relentless. In a heart-stopping instant, he plummeted over the precipice. The world turned into a blur of green and brown as branches and rocks whipped past him. His heart raced as adrenaline coursed through his veins. His body hit the jagged cliff face several times, each impact jarring his bones and tearing at his clothes. The pain was excruciating, but his survival instincts kicked in. He fought to stay conscious, desperately searching for something to grab onto. Finally, he crashed onto a narrow ledge, a sickening crunch resonating through the air as he landed awkwardly. Their laughter turned to stunned silence as the group peered over the cliff, fear etched on their faces.

Agonizing pain shot through Brian's leg, a clear signal that something was terribly wrong. Gritting his teeth, he glanced down to see his left leg skinned from his knees to his boot. It was bleeding, although not profusely. The uneven surface of the narrow ledge offered no relief as sharp rocks, slick with moss, dug into his back. His heart raced as panic set in, realizing the precariousness of his situation. He tried to move, but a wave of nausea overwhelmed him, forcing him to lie still and assess the extent of his injuries.

The ledge, which was only as large as his body, provided no room for self-examination. Brian could only rely on his gut feeling, which told him that the injuries were bad. He feared for his three friends above, who were unaware of his predicament, and especially his girlfriend, Roz. Brian and Roz had been dating since their first year at Young Harris, and their relationship had blossomed into a deep, committed love. Their arm-in-arm appearances were campus-famous, and they had even set a wedding date two years out. June 20th, Mia's birthday, would be the day they would start their new chapter together at the University of Georgia, where they planned to pursue their respective degrees. Mia in Horticulture and Brian in an undisclosed field.

Now, however, Brian's hopes for that future seemed uncertain. Lying on the ledge, unable to move, he couldn't help but remember the childhood pain of his tonsillectomy. The memory served as a reminder of the long recovery and the limitations it imposed.

Looking out across the valley, Brian admired the beauty of the verdant landscape that signaled spring. But amidst the beauty, he couldn't escape the reality of his dire situation. Any false move now could send him tumbling down the mountain to a sure death far below. Time seemed to stretch endlessly, and Brian wondered how he would ever reach the summit again. Yet, his determination and rugged toughness gave him a glimmer of hope. He knew he had to survive and reunite with his loved ones.

Above, the terrified shouts of his friends echoed as they peered over the edge of the steep cliff, their faces pale with fear. Brian's heart pounded in his chest, both from the sudden adrenaline rush caused by the fall and the dawning realization of the dire situation he now found himself in. The once inviting and harmless trail they had embarked on had transformed into a treacherous and life-threatening ordeal. The jagged rocks and sheer drops that surrounded them served as constant reminders of the imminent danger they were facing. In this high-stakes scenario, every second mattered, and their survival hinged on their ability to assess the situation quickly and respond with utmost agility and resourcefulness.

"Oh, God," Brian prayed in earnest, "Please help your humble servant. Only you can make a way for me now. I need your grace more than ever! Help me, dear Jesus."

With his heart pounding in his chest, Jake peered over the edge of the rocky cliff where his best friend, Brian, lay injured and unconscious below. Easily over fifty feet, the sheer drop was intimidating, with jagged rocks and boulders below. The sound of Brian's labored breathing echoed in Jake's ears, fueling his determination to reach him as quickly as possible. The urgency of the situation left no room for hesitation. Assessing the treacherous terrain ahead, Jake mentally prepared himself for the daunting descent. He took a deep breath, feeling the adrenaline coursing through his veins, and braced himself for the risky and physically demanding rescue mission that lay before him. Jake felt this moment was destined for him.

"Heavenly Father, you are my strength and hope," Jake prayed. "I give myself to you completely and pray for your will to be done in this situation. I must reach Brian and bring him back up safely."

Mia and Roz laid their hands on Jake and uttered

prayers for his safety.

The afternoon grew heavy with suspense for the four hikers and the uncertainty of Brian's situation as it weighed upon the minds of his three friends, Roz, Jake, and Mia.

Carefully, Jake, a seasoned mountaineer, began his slow, cautious climb down the rocky mountainside of Black Mountain. Each step was deliberate, his hands gripping the jagged rocks with white-knuckled intensity. His every step unearthed rock as they tumbled down the mountainside. The wind, which had a mind of its own at such altitudes, whipped around him, threatening to unbalance his precarious position. He could hear the distant calls of Mia and Roz above him, their voices a mix of encouragement and fear. Despite the adrenaline coursing through his veins, Jake remained focused, blocking out the distractions of the breathtaking view and the deafening silence of the mountain. The rough surface scraped against his palms, leaving behind small abrasions, but he ignored the pain, knowing that reaching his friend was of utmost importance. His muscles strained with the effort, and beads of sweat trickled down his forehead, despite the cool air that enveloped the towering peak. He calculated every movement, testing each foothold before shifting his weight, ensuring that each step brought him closer to his goal—reuniting with his friend and conquering the climb back up together.

In the heart-pounding tale of Jake's daring rescue mission, every step down the treacherous 50-foot mountainside brings back memories of his relentless football training. With each muscle in his body stretched and strained, his unwavering focus was solely on securing his friend Brian and ensuring their safe return. Amidst the dangerous descent, the jagged rocks test Jake's unwavering determination as he navigates them, willing himself not to succumb to the looming threat of doom. Even a cut on his finger cannot distract him from his mission, as he remains steadfast in his commitment to saving Brian, knowing that his friend would do the same for him.

As Jake carefully maneuvers down the rocky mountainside, he reflects on the countless hours spent on the football field, honing his physical strength and mental resilience. The grueling practices and intense drills prepared him for moments like these, instilling in him the discipline to push past his own limitations. Each step requires utmost caution, with the terrain presenting an array of potential hazards that could spell disaster with a single misstep.

Despite the physical strain and the distracting pain from his finger cut, Jake remains unwaveringly focused on his primary aim: rescuing Brian from their precarious situation. The minor injury serves as a constant reminder of the urgency of their predicament, fueling his determination to overcome any obstacles that stand in his path.

Jake's unwavering loyalty to his friend shines through as he selflessly puts Brian's safety above his own. He understands the gravity of the situation and knows that even the smallest lapse in concentration could have devastating consequences. He perseveres, drawing strength from the knowledge that Brian would do the same for him.

In this heart-stopping tale of courage and sacrifice, Jake's harrowing descent down the treacherous mountainside displays his unwavering determination and selflessness. Every step is a testament to the intense physical and mental training he has undergone, as well as the unbreakable bond of friendship that drives him forward. As he navigates the jagged rocks, the minor cut on his finger serves as a constant reminder of the risks they face. Yet, with his unwavering focus on Brian's safety, Jake continues his perilous journey, ready to face any challenges that come their way.

Jake could hear Roz shouting down to him from the cliff above. "Jake, please, please, please be careful. I love you, honey!" Mia yelled, her voice filled with worry and concern. She had always been protective of Jake, especially in situations where his safety was at risk.

Determined to keep his mind sharp, Jake continued to engage in conversation with his friend, Brian. Talking to Brian not only provided a welcome distraction, but it also helped to keep his mind alert and focused on the task at hand.

Jake reminisced about a humorous incident from their college days, hoping to lighten the tense atmosphere. "Hey, Buddy," he called to Brian, his voice laced with a touch of frivolity. "Remember that time at Young Harris when we went skating over in Blairsville and I started going out of control and hit the wall?" Jake asked, a faint smile playing on his lips.

Brian, his voice trembling slightly, responded, "Yes, I do, Jake. And you thought I was a bad skater?" His shaky response revealed the underlying anxiety both friends were feeling in the face of the perilous situation.

"Do you remember the old man that came to my aid and fixed me up?" Jake asked with humor.

"Yea," Brian responded. "I remember what a baby you were when he rubbed alcohol on your wound and put a bandage on it."

"We managed, Buddy, and we came through that night, okay." Jake said. "And you're gonna be O.K. Brian? It's your turn now. Stay strong; we'll help you get back on your feet."

As Jake descended, the distance to Brian slowly closed. He sees the pain etched on his friend's face, the injured leg, and the urgency in his eyes. Jake's heart raced with a mix of fear and determination. He knew that time was of the essence, and he couldn't afford to waste a single second. The treacherous terrain made the descent even more challenging, with loose rocks and steep cliffs threatening to send him plunging to his own demise. But Jake pushed forward, his mind focused solely on reaching his injured friend.

Finally, after what felt like an eternity, Jake reached the narrow ledge. He carefully maneuvered his body onto the precarious surface, his muscles burning with exertion. As he crouched beside his friend, he couldn't help but notice the sweat dripping down his own forehead, matching the perspiration on his friend's brow. The air was thick with tension, but Jake refused to let panic take hold of him.

"Hang in there, buddy," he said, his voice steady despite the adrenaline coursing through him. "I will get you out of here." He knew their lives depended on his actions, and he couldn't afford to falter now.

Pain and desperation filled his friend's response. "Jake, it's bad!" Brian exclaimed, his voice trembling with anguish. The gravity of the situation hit Jake like a ton of bricks, but he refused to let doubt cloud his judgment. He assessed his friend's injuries quickly, knowing that every second counted.

2

Spring Break has Arrived!

Everyone on campus was excited about spring break arriving. There was a crispness in the air, signaling the much-anticipated break from classes and academic responsibilities. As the days grew longer and the weather grew warmer, students could feel the energy building up in the atmosphere. The promise of two weeks of freedom from exams, papers, and lectures created a palpable sense of excitement among the student body. It was a time to recharge, relax, and engage in activities outside the confines of the campus. The anticipation of spring break was not just about the extended time off; it was also a reminder that the end of the semester was within reach. As students looked forward to the adventures and relaxation that awaited them, there was a sense of accomplishment and satisfaction knowing that they had almost made it through another challenging semester. Despite the cold weather still permeating campus, these young adults gladly welcomed spring and refused to be deterred.

Exhilaration washed over students as the break neared; plans for travel, home visits, or restful relaxation filled their minds. The campus buzzed with discussions of exotic destinations, road trips, and gatherings with friends and family. Spring break was not just a vacation; it was a well-deserved reward for the hard work and dedication that students had put into their studies. With each passing day, the excitement grew, and the countdown to the start of spring break became the focal point of conversations and daydreams.

Bad news arrived the day before of a tragic accident in the quaint mountain town of Blue Ridge, Georgia. The incident claimed the life of a promising sophomore at Young Harris College, a close-knit educational institution known for its vibrant student community. The unfortunate incident occurred while the victim, identified as Johnny Barkley, and his close friend, Roy Simpson, were indulging in their shared love for nature and adventure. They had embarked on a hiking expedition along the scenic Toccoa River, unaware that this excursion would soon turn into a devastating tragedy.

The serene beauty of the river's surroundings quickly shattered when Johnny Barkley slipped on a treacherous patch of terrain and tumbled into the icy waters below.

Shock and panic gripped Roy Simpson as he desperately tried to reach out and save his friend from the merciless current. However, the powerful, rapid river proved unforgiving, swiftly sweeping Johnny away before Roy's eyes. Distraught and helpless, Roy could only watch as his dear friend disappeared, carried downstream by the relentless force of the water.

Realizing the gravity of the situation, Roy immediately contacted 9-1-1 and soon the civil defense authorities and police in Blue Ridge arrived to launch a search and rescue operation for Johnny Barkley. The dedicated team of professionals promptly mobilized, braving the challenging conditions of the river to locate and retrieve the missing hiker. After an arduous three-mile search, they finally found Johnny's lifeless body, tragically entangled amidst the branches protruding from the riverbank.

The heart-wrenching news of Johnny's untimely demise reverberated across the Young Harris College campus, casting a somber cloud over the usually vibrant student community. Losing such a young, promising life devastated friends, classmates, and faculty members. The college provided grief counselors to support and comfort those affected as the entire campus grappled with the profound sadness of losing a cherished community member.

Following this devastating incident, the community of

Blue Ridge mourned Johnny Barkley, a vibrant young soul whose life ended so suddenly. The incident serves as a stark reminder of the unpredictable nature of the great outdoors and the importance of taking necessary precautions while engaging in adventurous activities. The memory of Johnny Barkley will forever remain in the hearts of those who knew and loved him, serving as a poignant reminder of the fragility of life and the need to cherish every moment.

When something of this magnitude happens, such as a natural disaster or a major economic crisis, there is a tendency of it dampening the spirits of those around. Consequences of such events are far-reaching, affecting individuals, communities, and society at large. The aftermath of a natural disaster, for instance, can leave people feeling devastated, helpless, and overwhelmed with grief. The destruction of homes, loss of loved ones, and the disruption of daily life can have a profound effect on the mental and emotional well-being of those affected. Similarly, a severe economic downturn can lead to widespread job loss, financial instability, and a sense of despair. The uncertainty and anxiety that come with such circumstances can weigh heavily on people's minds, making it difficult for them to maintain a positive outlook and find hope in the face of adversity. In these challenging times, it becomes crucial to provide support, empathy, and resources to help individuals and communities cope with the emotional toll and rebuild their lives.

Tomorrow morning, at the break of dawn, four close friends from the University, Brian, Mia, Jake, and Roz (Rosalyn) would depart for the start of the Appalachian Trail at Amicalola Falls State Park. This would mark the beginning of their long-awaited adventure of hiking a goodly portion of the Georgia trail during spring break.

The Appalachian Trail is a legendary footpath that stretches over 2,200 miles, spanning through 14 states from Georgia to Maine. Challenging terrain, breathtaking scenery, and a profound sense of accomplishment characterize it for those who conquer it.

The trail, known for its mystique and allure, captivates adventurers as they embark on this journey. An air of mystery and enchantment envelops them. The trail also holds many of its own secrets, gleaned from countless occurrences throughout the years. Generations have shared these stories, passed down from saints and sages, and whispered among families and friends. Tales of fear and terror, death, and tragic events have become intertwined with the very essence of d nature enthusiasts alike. Its winding paths lead through dense forests, towering mountains, and breathtaking landscapes. Traveling the trail, leaving a permanent mark on the collective mentality of those who will journey forward, creates a certain mysterious view for all involved.

The night before their journey, while having a final planning session, Jake Sutton shared one legend of the trail with the group of four.

"My father used to tell me about Mishipeshu, an old Cherokee Indian legend about a mysterious underwater panther that lives near streams of water and dwells within the depths. According to the legend, Mishipeshu is a fearsome creature with the body of a wild feline and the scales of a serpent. It is said to possess incredible power and is believed to guard the sacred waters, controlling the flow of life itself. The legend warns of the chilling sound that emanates from Mishipeshu, a bone-chilling noise that can send shivers down your spine. It is a sound that must not be underestimated, for it can entice unsuspecting souls into its clutches, forever trapping them in its watery domain. As we embark on this mission, we must remain vigilant and heed the wisdom of the legend, ensuring that we do not fall victim to Mishipeshu's seductive call."

Roz chimed in with concern. "Jake Sutton! I am surprised at you trying to upset us and bring fear into the trip even before we begin!"

"Roz, you know I love you dearly, but I just had to share that story. It's going to be an endless trip unless we loosen up and enjoy it with a few stories from the past." Jake said with compassion.

Jake Sutton, age 22 and the oldest of the four, had been on different sections of the trail before with his dad, but it had been three years now since their last trek, which took them into North Carolina. From his father, a very skilled engineer with a large Atlanta firm, Jake gained a lot of knowledge about hiking and the outdoors. Mr. Sutton, Jake's dad, had been Jake's scoutmaster while he worked on his Eagle Scout award, which is the highest honor for Boy Scouts. Under his father's guidance, Jake learned all the fundamentals of hiking safety, preparedness, and what to do in extreme situations. From packing the right gear and food to understanding how to navigate using a compass and map, Jake had gained a wealth of practical skills and knowledge that made him a confident and capable hiker. He knew the importance of staying hydrated, recognizing potential hazards on the trail, and taking necessary precautions to ensure his safety. Jake's dad had also taught him how to build a shelter, start a fire, and administer basic first aid skills that could prove invaluable in emergency situations. With his extensive training and experience, Jake felt ready to take on new challenges and explore the beauty of the trail once again.

Jake, a talented athlete, was not only a star on the basketball court but also the quarterback for his high school football team. His exceptional skills led him to set new state records for passing, making him a celebrated figure in the world of high school sports. Jake's leadership abilities were obvious as he guided his team to the state finals three years in a row, showcasing his determination and strategic thinking on the field. Despite his achievements in various sports, football was his genuine passion. He dedicated countless hours to perfecting his skills and studying the game, always striving for greatness. Jake made thorough preparations for his upcoming spring break hike on the Appalachian Trail. He meticulously planned every aspect of the trip; from the route they would take to the gear they would need. Passionate about sharing his enthusiasm for the journey, Jake tirelessly discussed the adventure with his eager companions, Mia, Roz, and Brian. Their excitement grew as they listened to Jake's detailed explanations and saw his genuine enthusiasm for the trip. With all the preparations in place, the four friends were ready to embark on this thrilling adventure together.

Jake's girlfriend was Rosalyn Butler, a petite and exquisite young 19-year-old from Silver Springs, Florida. Rosalyn, affectionately called Roz, was not only stunning but also incredibly talented and driven. She had an impressive athletic background, having achieved remarkable success in swimming by winning two state championships for the high dive. Her dedication and hard work extended beyond sports; she also excelled academically. Roz was a star student and achieved the highest honor of being named the Valedictorian of her graduating class. Her love for learning was clear through her commitment to her studies, particularly towards earning her registered nursing degree. However, Roz's ambitions didn't stop there. She had big plans to further her medical career by pursuing a P.A. degree (Physician Assistant). Roz's exceptional intelligence, unwavering determination, and infectious enthusiasm for education ensured her greatness in her chosen field. Roz, as she was affectionately called, had been her class Valedictorian and loved school. She was also a talker, letting no one get a word into her conversations. Her friends always chided her about that. Roz really did not care about hiking, camping, backpacking and such, but she loved Jake Sutton and would follow him anywhere he led.

People knew Mia Spencer as the class clown, always bringing laughter and joy to those around her. Despite her playful nature, she was also a dedicated student who had recently turned twenty-one-years old. With her graduation approaching in May, she was excited to receive her well-deserved honors degree in Horticulture. Plants and trees had always fascinated Mia, and she saw the upcoming hike as an opportunity to explore the great variety of flora along the Appalachian Trail (A.T.). Her passion for horticulture was clear, as she had already secured a fellowship at the University of Georgia for the upcoming fall semester. At UGA, Mia planned to continue her studies in Horticulture, eager to expand her knowledge and skills in this field. However, her ambitions didn't stop there. Mia dreamed of one day working as a missionary in a foreign third-world country, using her expertise in horticulture to make a positive impact on the lives of others. With her loving and outgoing personality, Mia was truly an all-people girl who had a bright future ahead of her. She grew up in Macon, a sizable town just 80 miles south of Atlanta on Interstate 75.

Mia's grandmother, Grandma Hastings, has been a significant influence on Mia's passion for horticulture. Ever since Mia's grandfather passed away, Grandma Hastings has been living with their family. Mia's dad wanted her to be comfortable and private, so he fixed up a building in their backyard and made a lovely apartment for her.

Grandma Hastings not only possessed a green thumb but also had a great sense of humor, which might explain Mia's playful personality. Behind her suite, there was a plot of land where Grandma Hastings dedicated countless hours during the summer, meticulously crafting a garden that was truly awe-inspiring. The garden boasted a variety of crops, including cabbage, cucumbers, rows of sweet potatoes, green beans, and corn. However, it was the butter beans, Mia's absolute favorite, that Grandma Hastings nurtured with extra care and attention.

Mrs. Hastings, better known as Me-Ma to Mia, was a passionate gardener who took great pleasure in teaching her granddaughter the art of gardening. From a young age, Mia would spend countless hours by her side, learning the ins and outs of cultivating a thriving garden. Me-Ma would patiently guide Mia through each step of the process, starting with the meticulous preparation of the soil. Together, they would dig, weed, and enrich the earth, ensuring a fertile foundation for their plants.

Once the soil was ready, Me-Ma would show Mia how to sow the seeds carefully, explaining the importance of proper spacing and depth. With each season, Mia's knowledge and skills grew, as Me-Ma instilled in her the importance of constant care and attention that a garden demanded. Mia learned to water the plants diligently, noting their individual needs and adjusting her watering schedule accordingly. Me-Ma also emphasized the significance of organic gardening, teaching Mia about natural methods to control pests and diseases without harmful chemicals. Mia became adept at identifying and removing harmful insects, as well as implementing organic solutions like companion planting and homemade pest sprays.

As the fruits of their labor ripened, Me-Ma would teach Mia the art of harvesting, showing her how to recognize the signs of readiness in each vegetable. Together, they would pick the vegetables at their peak, ensuring the freshest and most flavorful produce for their table. Thanks to Me-Ma's patient guidance and expertise, Mia developed a firm knowledge and love for gardening that would stay with her throughout her life. The bond formed between Mia and her Me-Ma in the garden was not just about growing plants, but about nurturing a connection to nature and passing down a treasured tradition from one generation to the next.

Me-Ma, Mia's grandmother, taught her many lessons. She was a wise and caring woman who had a wealth of knowledge and experiences to share. One of the most valuable lessons she taught Mia was the importance of perseverance. Me-Ma faced many challenges throughout her life, but she never gave up. She taught Mia that no matter how difficult the circumstances are; it is important to keep pushing forward and never lose sight of your goals.

Another lesson she learned from her was the importance of kindness and compassion. Me-Ma always helped others and showed Mia that a minor act of kindness can make a big difference in someone's life. She taught her to treat everyone with respect and empathy, regardless of their background or circumstances. Me-Ma also instilled in Mia the value of hard work and determination. She believed that success comes from putting in the effort and staying committed to your dreams. She taught the young apprentice to set high standards for herself and to always strive for excellence in everything. Me-Ma's lessons have had a profound impact on Mia's life, shaping her into the person she is today.

One thing was certain: Mia also loved Brian Foster. She loved him deeply, with every fiber of her being. Their love was a force that transcended time and distance. Mia understood that their love would face challenges, as she had plans for her future. She was determined to pursue her dreams and aspirations, which included completing her fellowship at Georgia and then embarking on a mission field somewhere in the world. Mia's desire was to use her knowledge and skills to empower other countries to grow crops that would help feed their people. Compassion and a strong sense of purpose filled her heart. She knew her path would require sacrifice and dedication, but she will go to great lengths to make a positive impact on the lives of others. With Brian by her side, supporting her every step of the way, Mia felt invincible. Their love gave her the strength and motivation to overcome any obstacles that might come their way. Together, they were a force to be reckoned with, ready to make a difference in the world.

Mia's interest in helping third-world countries came from a church presentation by a middle-aged minister one night. The church congregation invited the minister, Reverend Johnson, to shed light on the dire need for clean water in Uganda. As he passionately spoke about the lack of access to safe drinking water and the devastating consequences it had on the people's health and well-being, Mia's heart went out to the individuals and families affected. Reverend Johnson explained the arduous process of digging wells in Uganda, highlighting the significant impact it could have on improving their lives. Mesmerized by his words and deeply moved by the plight of the Ugandan people, Mia's concern for their well-being intensified. She felt a powerful urge to act and make a difference in their lives. Inspired by the presentation, Mia embarked on a journey to explore ways she could contribute to the cause and help bring clean water to those in need. In fact, Mia, a dedicated and compassionate student at Lake Weir High School, had eagerly volunteered to go on a life-changing mission team with the minister during the following summer. With her junior year just around the corner, Mia saw this as the perfect opportunity to make a positive impact on the world and broaden her horizons. Excited but also aware of the responsibilities that came with this endeavor, Mia embarked on a journey to prepare herself for the mission. Foremost, she had to secure a passport, as the mission would have taken place in a foreign country. Determined to contribute meaningfully, Mia knew she had to travel light and pack only the essentials. This meant Mia carefully chose the items for her journey, leaving behind anything unnecessary. Mia took it upon herself to raise funds for her trip, understanding that financial support was crucial to making this mission a reality. She organized various fundraising activities, such as bake sales, car washes, and community events, in order to gather the funds.

Two meetings with the team were mandatory for the team to bond, plan, and prepare for the challenges they would face during their time abroad. Together, they discussed logistics, cultural sensitivities, and the goals they hoped to achieve. Through these sessions, Mia formed friendships and built a support system that would prove invaluable on this transformative journey. With her passport secured, essentials packed, funds raised, and sessions attended, Mia was ready to embark on a summer adventure that would shape her perspective and leave a lasting impact on those she would encounter.

The trip to Uganda would change Mia's life forever. Little did she know that the experience she was about to embark on would leave an indelible mark on her soul. In Uganda's impoverished villages, Mia encountered a reality she could never have imagined. The extreme poverty that she witnessed, with families struggling to meet even their most basic needs, struck a chord deep within her heart. Witnessing these people's harsh living conditions shattered her heart. In that moment, Mia knew she could no longer stand by idly and do nothing. The trip ignited a fire within her to take action and make a difference in the lives of those less fortunate. Mia became determined to use her voice and resources to create a positive impact on the world. From that day forward, she dedicated her life to helping those in need, advocating for change, and making a difference in any way she could. The trip to Uganda was not just a journey, but a turning point in Mia's life, guiding her on a path of compassion, empathy, and unwavering determination.

Mia's heart was as pure as the driven snow. From a young age, she exuded an innate kindness and compassion that touched the lives of those around her. Her selflessness knew no bounds, as she consistently put the needs and happiness of others before her own. Mia's kindness was remarkable; she always helped those in need, friends and strangers alike.

Personal gain or recognition did not motivate her actions, but by the simple desire to make the world a better place. This purity of heart and unwavering goodness radiated from her, leaving an indelible impact on all who had the privilege of crossing paths with her. Mia's heart was a beacon of light, illuminating the darkness and reminding us of all the power of love and compassion in our lives.

And then there was Brian Foster. Brian was a soft-hearted fellow who had left the farm in Telfair County, Georgia, and had fared well at Young Harris, the college each of the four friends attended. It had been quite a change for Brian, as it was the farthest from home he had ever been. Pursuing his passion for helping others, Brian had chosen Sociology as his major and planned to pursue a career in social work after graduation. He knew it would be challenging, but he was determined to make a difference in people's lives. Brian had made a promise to his girlfriend, Mia, that he would do his best to find work in the Athens, Georgia area, near the University of Georgia, so they could continue to be together. He hoped that his farming skills, honed from growing up on a farm, would somehow come in handy during their upcoming hike, although the other three friends could not quite see how. Brian remained optimistic and believed that his diverse background would contribute to the group's journey in unexpected ways.

Farming had been Brian's life from an early age. Growing up on a small family farm in rural Iowa, he spent countless hours in the fields alongside his father, learning the ins and outs of agriculture. Whether it was tending to the crops, feeding the livestock, or fixing machinery, Brian was always eager to lend a hand. His father, a hardworking and resilient man, instilled in him the values of perseverance and dedication. As a result, Brian's hands had become calloused from years of toiling under the scorching sun and enduring the harsh elements. Despite the physical toll, he understood the importance of their work in providing for their family and contributing to their community's food supply. Their farm provided more than just income for them; it was a way of life.

Leaving home for college was a welcome respite for Brian. After years of living in a small town and feeling like he was constantly under the watchful eyes of his neighbors, he was eager to experience a new sense of freedom and independence. The thought of being able to make his own decisions and explore new opportunities was exhilarating. Brian was excited about the prospect of meeting new people from diverse backgrounds and engaging in intellectual discussions. College offered him the chance to pursue his passion for learning and expand his horizons beyond what he had previously thought possible. College would be where he would meet the love of his life, Mia. With her horticultural interests and Brian's love of farming, it was a match made in heaven. The two were synonymous.

The four friends had formed an unbreakable bond during their time at Young Harris College. Over four years, they had shared countless memories and experiences together. Whether attending classes, taking part in extracurricular activities, or simply hanging out on campus, they always appeared as a tight-knit group. Their double-dates were legendary, often becoming the topic of conversation among their peers. The small college, in the serene surroundings of North Georgia, offered a close-knit community where everyone seemed to know each other.

Nestled in the picturesque foothills of the Blue Ridge mountains, the campus provided a breathtaking backdrop for their adventures. As they navigated through their college years, the four friends became known as the dynamic quartet, leaving a lasting impression on the campus community. They were actively involved in their chapter of Campus Crusade for Christ and did volunteer work for the organization throughout the area. The four friends, Mia, Brian, Jake, and Roz, dedicated their time and efforts to making a positive impact in their community.

One of their regular activities was visiting local nursing homes once each month. They brought joy and companionship to older adult residents, brightening their days with their presence. Brian, a talented musician, would strum his guitar while the others joined in singing old favorite hymns. Their harmonious voices filled the halls, creating a warm and uplifting atmosphere for everyone in the nursing home. The residents eagerly awaited their monthly visits, cherishing the moments of connection and the beautiful music that brought back cherished memories. Through their dedication and the power of music, Mia, Brian, Jake, and Roz could make a difference in the lives of the nursing home residents, bringing smiles and a sense of belonging to those who needed it most.

The folks in Young Harris, Georgia, a quaint, small town nestled in the beautiful Appalachian Mountains, far from the bustling city life of an Atlanta or Nashville, have long attracted many students to the area because of its pristine mountainous location. With its serene and picturesque surroundings, Young Harris offers a unique and tranquil environment that is perfect for those seeking a break from the fast-paced urban lifestyle. The town's proximity to nature trails, hiking routes, and breathtaking viewpoints makes it an ideal destination for outdoor enthusiasts and adventure seekers. Young Harris boasts a

strong sense of community, where neighbors come together to support local businesses, cultural events, and educational institutions. The town's charm and warm hos-
pitality make it a welcoming place for students who can
enjoy the benefits of a close-knit community while pursuing their academic goals. Whether it's exploring the natural wonders of the surrounding mountains or immersing oneself in the town's rich history and culture, Young
Harris offers a unique experience that captures the hearts
of all who visit.

In this beautiful setting, Roz, Jake, Mia, and Brian set
out to conquer a portion of the Appalachian Trail (A.T.)
together. The A.T. winds through stunning landscapes,
including lush forests, scenic mountain ranges, and picturesque meadows. Two young couples, Roz and Jake, and
Mia and Brian, possessing the abilities and adventurous
spirits of many before them, rise early on the day of departure and go through their checklists. They pack their
sturdy hiking boots, lightweight tents, warm sleeping bags,
and ample supplies of food and water. Excitement fills the
air as they expect the challenges and rewards that lie ahead
on their journey along the A.T. They were ready to leave
behind the comforts of their everyday lives and immerse
themselves in the raw and untamed wilderness. With each
step they would take, they would follow in the footsteps

of countless hikers who had come before them, joining a community of nature enthusiasts who sought solace and adventure on the trail. The friends were eager to embrace the challenges that awaited them, knowing that this would be a transformative experience that would test their limits and forge lifelong memories.

3

The Departure

Spring was always beautiful around the Young Harris campus. The rolling hills displayed vibrant trilliums and daffodils, creating a picturesque scenery. As the sun graced the sky, there were hints of warmth that embraced the air, with temperatures typically reaching into the pleasant mid-fifties. It was during this time that four adventurous souls, Roz, Jake, Brian, and Mia, embarked on an exciting journey on the Appalachian Trail. With high spirits and backpacks filled with essentials, Roz, Jake, Brian, and Mia prepared for a thrilling two-week stint on the Appalachian Trail.

The present is manageable, but the future is uncertain. Life can change on a dime. We often navigate through the difficulties of life, trying to make the best decisions and plans for our future. However, despite our efforts, there are many factors that can completely alter our path and transform our lives in unexpected ways. It is this unpredictability that adds a sense of mystery and excitement to our journey, but it can also bring about feelings of anxiety and unease. The future holds infinite possibilities, both positive and negative, and it is up to us to embrace the uncertainty and adapt to whatever comes our way.

These four adventurous hikers had meticulously planned their two-week hiking expedition, carefully mapping out the route they would take and the landmarks they hoped to encounter along the way. With their backpacks packed and their spirits high, they embarked on their journey with an air of excitement and anticipation. Little did they know, however, that the rugged terrain and unpredictable weather would present them with unforeseen challenges and tests of their resilience. As they ventured further into the wilderness, they would soon come face to face with steep cliffs, dense forests, and treacherous river crossings. The journey they had embarked upon would not only test their physical endurance but also their mental fortitude. With each passing day, they would discover new depths of strength within themselves and forge an unbreakable bond with one another. The unknown that lay ahead would push them to their limits and transform them into seasoned explorers, forever changed by the awe-inspiring beauty and unforgiving nature of the wilderness.

Roz was the first to wake up at 5:00 a.m. in the dorm

room she shared with Mia. Get up, Mia, you sleepyhead!

"Roz, could this wait? Mia inquired. I was enjoying a wonderful dream and didn't want it to end."

"No, it can't wait, Mia," Roz urgently exclaimed. Her voice filled with determination and a hint of frustration. "You know how meticulously we have all planned for this trip. We have created a detailed itinerary and have poured our hearts into making this adventure unforgettable. So, please, get up, take your shower, and get ready."

Roz's words resonated with a sense of urgency, emphasizing the importance of sticking to the meticulously crafted plan. The trip was carefully planned down to the smallest details, ensuring that every moment was accounted for. The meeting time with the rest of the group in the south end parking lot was set at the crack of dawn, precisely at six a.m. There was no room for sleeping in or delays. The thought of deviating from the schedule seemed out of the question.

Roz's stern tone reflected the determination and dedication both she and Mia had invested in making this trip a success. The anticipation of the adventure ahead and the desire to make the most out of every minute fueled their motivation. It was clear that Roz's urgency stemmed from a shared commitment to experiencing everything they had planned, leaving no opportunity wasted.

Mia, still cocooned in her warm and comfortable bed, felt a mix of reluctance and excitement. She knew that succumbing to the temptation of a few more minutes of sleep could jeopardize the carefully curated plan they had worked so hard to put together. With a deep breath, she resolved to push aside any thoughts of laziness and embrace the adventure that awaited her outside the confines of her cozy bedroom.

As the alarm clock continued to tick away, the weight of the impending departure settled on Mia's shoulders. She knew that time was of the essence, and she had to rise to the occasion. With a newfound determination, Mia threw off her covers and swung her legs over the side of the bed. The warmth of her slippers was quickly replaced by the cold touch of the floor as she made her way towards the bathroom.

The sound of water cascading from the showerhead echoed through the small bathroom, creating a sense of urgency and anticipation. As the water washed away the remnants of sleep, Mia felt a surge of energy coursing through her veins. She knew that every minute counted, and she had to be ready to seize the day.

With her heart pounding and her mind focused, Mia stood before the bathroom mirror. She took a moment to gather herself, her reflection revealing a mix of determination and excitement. The adventure that awaited her was just within reach, and she was ready to embrace it with open arms.

As Mia finished getting ready, she couldn't help but feel grateful for Roz's insistence and unwavering dedication. Their shared passion for exploration and discovery had brought them to this point, and Mia knew that together, they would make this trip an unforgettable experience. With a final glance in the mirror, Mia took a deep breath, ready to face the challenges and wonders that awaited her on this meticulously planned journey.

"You can really be a pain sometimes," Mia said, playfully teasing her companion. "We've got all day to get there, Roz. What could be so important to wake up before the chickens?"

Roz chuckled, her eyes sparkling with excitement. "Oh, Mia, you know me! I just can't contain my enthusiasm for what lies ahead," she exclaimed. "This trip is not just about reaching our destination; it's about the journey itself. The early start ensures that we have ample time to immerse ourselves in the surroundings, savor every moment, and capture the breathtaking beauty of nature along the way."

Mia couldn't help but smile at Roz's infectious spirit. She knew that her friend had meticulously planned every detail of this adventure, researching the best routes, identifying hidden gems, and even arranging encounters with local experts. Roz's dedication to creating a rich and meaningful experience for both and the guys was truly commendable.

As they stepped outside, the crisp morning air greeted them, invigorating their senses. The sun had just begun to rise, casting a warm golden glow over the landscape. Mia could already feel the anticipation building up inside her, knowing that this trip would be unlike anything she had ever experienced before.

With their backpacks filled with essentials and their cameras ready to capture every moment, Mia and Roz set off on their journey to meet up with Jake and Brian. The path ahead was unknown, but their shared passion and unwavering determination would guide them through any challenges they might face.

As they walked side by side, Mia couldn't help but feel grateful for Roz's unwavering support and insistence on exploring the world together. They were not just travel companions; they were kindred spirits, united by a thirst for adventure and a curiosity about the world that knew no bounds.

As they ventured deeper into the unknown, Mia knew that this trip would be a turning point in their lives. It would not only provide them with unforgettable memories but also strengthen their bond and ignite a lifelong love for exploration. They were ready to embrace whatever wonders and challenges lay ahead, confident that their shared passion would guide them through it all. "You know what the guys are like, Mia," Roz replied. Before dark, they plan to reach the Hawk Mountain shelter; they're prepared and enthusiastic."

"Okay, I'm coming," Mia snapped. I need to quickly shower and double-check my backpack for anything I might forget.

"Mia, that's a good idea," Roz confirmed. I need to quickly add a few more things to my backpack, so let's hurry."

Jake and Brian were eating a snack in their dorm room while discussing the day ahead.

Brian initiated the conversation by inquiring, "Jake, have you gathered all your belongings?"

"Just hold on there, Buddy." Jake offered. "You've got too many questions for me this early in the morning. Don't you know me better than that? You know how prepared I usually am. I stayed up until around 12:30 a.m. getting my stuff ready. Where were you? In the bed since 9:30 p.m."

Jake continued. "I'm glad that somebody has taken the time to make sure everything was ready to go."

"O.k., Superman! Should have known that you would have everything under control. That's why I love you so much, Bud. You always think ahead of me and prepare for the smallest of details," Brian said.

Around 5:30 a.m., Jake called for Brian to follow him out to the parking lot so they could begin packing in his Ford F-150 pickup. Every inch of space would have to be used for all four backpacks to fit, along with a few other amenities. So, the two of them made their way to the truck in the darkly lit parking lot behind their dorm. Jake, always the planner, had parked his truck under a streetlight. Who would have thought it? Brian whispered to himself.

The girls arrived around 6 a.m. and handed Zack and Brian their suitcases and gave their boyfriends a big hug and a kiss.

"Ready to go, girls?" Brian asked.

"We're ready," Mia smiled. "I'm excited, but why did we have to leave so early?"

Jake insisted: "Mia, we've got over sixty-five miles to drive to reach Amicalola Falls State Park. We then must secure our parking space for a two-week period, talk with the park officials, and sign the hiking register."

"O.K., O.K.," Mia Shrugged. "I can tell that it's going to be a long day!"

The Appalachian Trail, stretching over 2,100 miles

from Georgia to Maine, is a dream for outdoor enthusiasts like Roz, Jake, Brian, and Mia. After months of planning and anticipation, their adventure was about to begin. They had meticulously packed their backpacks with essential gear, including tents, sleeping bags, cooking utensils, and enough food to sustain them on the trail. Excitement filled the air as they prepared to embark on this challenging journey through the breathtaking landscapes and rugged terrain of the Appalachian Mountains.

Roz, a nature lover and semi-experienced hiker, had been eagerly awaiting this moment. She knew that spring was the perfect time to hike the trail, with its blooming wildflowers, fresh green foliage, and comfortable temperatures. The group had chosen the two-week period to immerse themselves in the beauty and serenity of the trail, allowing ample time for exploration and enjoying the tranquility of nature. Jake had even placed a couple of days' rest into the schedule, just in care. They had carefully mapped out their route, planning to cover a sizable portion of the trail, taking in its most scenic sections and notable landmarks.

With their backpacks strapped on and hiking boots laced up, Mia and Roz, two college students, stood in the south end parking lot while the guys did the packing. They were embarking on a hiking adventure and had meticulously planned their trip to Amicalola Falls State Park, about an hour away. The south end parking lot near the boy's dorm was their designated meeting spot with their friends Brian and Jake. Jake's trusty Ford F-150 would transport them to their destination.

Their cheerful singing and laughter during the drive showed the group's excitement and anticipation of the day ahead. As they journeyed, Jake, known for his attention to detail, inquired about a small rope he had asked Roz to bring. Roz assured him she had packed it and even found the perfect spot for it. However, Jake's lack of trust in her seemed to bother Roz, but she playfully defended herself, questioning if she had ever let him down before. Mia, amused by the banter between Roz and Jake, interjected with her sarcasm, commenting on their complaints at such an early hour. Jake, in response, couldn't help but start singing "Oh, what a beautiful morning" to emphasize his positive outlook on the day. Mia teasingly questioned his choice of song at such an early hour, to which Jake suggested she should try it. Excitement, camaraderie, and playful banter filled the atmosphere as the group neared their destination.

Excitement and anticipation filled the air as the group embarked on their journey. Their cheerful singing and laughter during the drive set the tone for the day ahead.

Each member of the group had their own unique personality, and their interactions made the journey even more enjoyable.

Jake, known for his meticulousness, couldn't help but inquire about a small rope he had asked Roz to bring. He wanted to ensure that everything was in order for the day's activities. Roz assured him she had packed it and even found the perfect spot for it. However, Jake's lack of trust bothered Roz, but she playfully defended herself, reminding him she had never let him down before.

Mia, the observer of the group, found great amusement in the banter between Roz and Jake. She couldn't help but interject with her sarcasm, commenting on their complaints at such an early hour. Her playful teasing added to the camaraderie of the group, creating a lighthearted atmosphere.

In response to Mia's comment, Jake couldn't resist displaying his positive outlook on the day. He spontaneously started singing, "Oh, what a beautiful morning," emphasizing his excitement for the adventure that lay ahead. Mia, teasingly questioning his choice of song at such an early hour, prompted Jake to suggest she try it too, further adding to the playful banter within the group.

As the group approached their destination, excitement, camaraderie, and playful banter filled the atmosphere.

The journey had brought them closer together, and they couldn't wait to embark on the day's activities. Their cheerful singing and laughter continued, setting the stage for an unforgettable adventure.

Roz recounted a fascinating and harrowing tale from her childhood. She vividly described an incident that occurred when she was just a curious four-year-old. According to Roz, she found herself lost in the dense woods behind her family's home. As she narrated the story, it became apparent that the experience left an impression on her. The dense foliage, towering trees, and eerie silence of the forest created a sense of fear and uncertainty that is hard to forget. Despite her tender age, Roz navigated her way through the unfamiliar terrain, eventually finding her way back home. Her recollection of this childhood adventure serves as a reminder of the resilience and resourcefulness she possessed, even at such an early age.

Jake: "And you told us that story for what purpose? That's not the story we need to tell when we are about to take a two-week trek on the Appalachian Trail (A.T.)! We should focus on preparing ourselves mentally and physically for the challenges ahead, not dwelling on negative experiences."

With a smile, Roz offered Jake her reasoning, simply stating that she had believed the event would be entertaining for everyone present.

Brian: "Exactly, Roz. It's important for us to maintain a positive outlook and embrace the adventure that awaits us on the A.T. We shouldn't let any experiences discourage us. Instead, let's focus on the beautiful landscapes, the sense of accomplishment we will feel, and the camaraderie we will build during our two-week trek."

Together, the group realizes the importance of maintaining a positive mindset as they embark on their journey. They understand that the A.T. is a renowned trail that offers breathtaking scenery, unique challenges, and an opportunity for personal growth. By leaving behind any negativity and embracing the excitement and possibilities, they are ready to make the most of their upcoming adventure.

4

The Trail Awaits!

The entrance to Amicalola Falls State Park is near Dawsonville, Georgia. The park is in the southern Appalachian Mountains and covers an area of approximately 829 acres. Amicalola Falls State Park's stunning natural beauty, including the magnificent Amicalola Falls—the tallest waterfall in the Southeastern United States, cascading 729 feet—makes it famous. The park offers a range of recreational activities for visitors to enjoy, such as hiking, camping, fishing, and picnicking. It serves as the southern terminus of the famous Appalachian Trail, making it a popular starting point for hikers embarking on this iconic long-distance trail.

Its rich history spans centuries, with origins dating back to ancient civilizations. Various cultures have influenced the region, including those of indigenous peoples, colonial powers, and immigrant communities. From monumental architectural structures to intricate works of art, the historical remnants showcase the cultural heritage of the area. The region has witnessed significant events, including wars, revolutions, and the rise and fall of empires. Exploring the historical artifacts and narratives provides a deeper understanding of the region's past and its impact on the present.

Some twenty odd miles away is the beautiful city of Dahlonega, in Lumpkin County, Georgia. Dahlonega's fame comes from its role as the site of Georgia's first gold rush. The city holds great significance in American history, as it marked the beginning of the gold rush in the southeast region. During the gold rush, which occurred in the early 19th century, prospectors meticulously panned streams along the Appalachian Trail (A.T.), resulting in the discovery of a remarkable amount of gold. This precious metal played a crucial role in shaping the economy and development of the region. Today, Dahlonega proudly showcases its gold mining heritage through the Georgia Gold Museum, which provides visitors with a fascinating insight into the history and significance of gold mining in the area. Dahlonega is also home to North Georgia College, a renowned institution offering excellent educational opportunities.

The entrance to Amicalola Falls State Park was quite underwhelming as the team arrived during the early days of Spring, mid-April. The once vibrant trees had shed their leaves during the fall and winter months, leaving a somewhat barren landscape. Undeterred, they made their way through the check-in point and immediately began ascending a steep paved road that led to the Amicalola Lodge. Perched atop the mountain overlooking the magnificent falls, the lodge offered breathtaking views and a sense of serenity. Among the group, Jake and Mia were the only ones who had visited the park before, giving them a sense of familiarity and confidence in navigating the area. In fact, Jake had even arranged with the park officials to leave his truck in one of the Lodge's parking spaces for the duration of our two-week hike. While Jake went inside to complete the arrangements with the lodge staff, the rest eagerly unloaded their gear and began preparing themselves for the adventure that awaited.

Jake, a seasoned hiker, soon returned to the group and eagerly grabbed his gear, which comprised a sturdy backpack, a comfortable sleeping bag, his canteen, and essential camping supplies. As they gathered at the trailhead, the group formed a circle, creating a sense of unity and anticipation. Brian, a devout believer, took on the role of spiritual leader and offered a heartfelt prayer for God's protection throughout their journey. With humble words, he implored, "Dear God, we humbly ask for your blessings and guidance as we embark on this incredible adventure. May your presence always be with us, providing us with strength, wisdom, and protection. We pray for joy and excitement on this journey, allowing us to fully experience the wonders of your creation. As we dedicate ourselves to you, may we fulfill your divine will in our lives. Amen."

The dangers ahead on the trail could be enormous and depend upon the group's preparedness. It is crucial for hikers to assess thoroughly the potential risks they may encounter before embarking on their journey. Hikers must consider factors such as extreme weather, treacherous terrain, and wildlife encounters. Limited access to medical help in remote areas causes hikers possessing the knowledge and supplies for emergency situations. Proper navigation skills and equipment are essential to avoid getting lost. Adequate physical fitness and stamina are also vital, as hiking trails often require endurance and strength to overcome challenges along the way. Prior research and planning can mitigate these dangers, ensuring a safe and enjoyable hiking experience for all members of the group.

Ancient tales of creatures permeate stories circulating around the Appalachian Trail and those who have hiked its rugged path. These tales, passed down through generations, speak of mysterious beings that inhabit the dense forests and remote wilderness areas along the trail. Hikers and locals alike recount encounters with creatures such as Bigfoot, the legendary ape-like creature said to roam the mountains, and the Mothman, a winged humanoid said to possess supernatural abilities. Other stories tell of encounters with ghostly apparitions, shapeshifters, and mythical creatures that defy explanation. While many dismiss these tales as mere folklore, there are those who swear by their veracity, attributing strange occurrences and unexplained phenomena to these elusive beings. The allure of the unknown and the possibility of encountering these creatures add an element of excitement and intrigue to the already challenging and awe-inspiring journey along the Appalachian Trail.

There are also mystical aspects of the trail shared by many hikers before that one should know. These mystical experiences often stem from the profound sense of connection with nature that the trail provides. Hikers have reported feeling a deep spiritual bond with the surrounding wilderness, as if they are tapping into a hidden energy or ancient wisdom. Some have even claimed to have encountered spiritual beings or heard whispers of ancient tales while trekking through the dense forests. These mystical encounters can be incredibly transformative, offering hikers a chance to reflect on their place in the world and gain a heightened sense of awareness. It is important for prospective hikers to be open to these mystical possibilities and embrace the potential for spiritual growth along the trail.

The team felt prepared. For two straight months, the two couples met and walked two miles each evening before dinner. They followed a strict routine, ensuring that they would be physically fit and mentally focused on the upcoming challenge. Their dedication was unwavering as they pushed themselves to meet their fitness goals. Rain or shine, they laced up their sneakers and hit the pavement, determined to improve their endurance and stamina. These daily walks not only improved their physical health but also served as a bonding activity for the couples. As they strolled along the scenic route, they shared stories, laughed, and encouraged each other, creating a strong sense of camaraderie. With each passing day, their confidence grew, and they truly believed that they were ready to take on any obstacle that came their way. Their consistent and disciplined approach to their training regimen was a testament to their commitment and determination. As they embarked on the upcoming challenge, they carried with them the memories of those evening walks, knowing that their hard work and preparation would pay off.

The four friends made their way to the A.T. trailhead. The scent of fresh pine and the sounds of birds chirping filled the air as they took their first steps onto the Appalachian Trail. Ahead of them lay countless miles of untamed wilderness, challenging ascents, and breathtaking vistas. They were ready to embrace the adventure and create memories that would last a lifetime.

As they headed up the 2.8-mile trek to Springer Mountain, the air was brisk and cool. The junior team had prepared well, however, and had packed the necessary clothing for the journey. Mia, the would-be horticulturist, found the abundance of plant species along the trail captivating. She marveled at the Spring Beauty, one of the earliest bloomers, with its petite flowers and delicate pink and white petals. Mia observed that these beautiful flowers mostly thrived in the low, moist, wooded areas of the trail. As she continued, she couldn't help but notice the promising growth of Fire Pinks and Flame Azaleas, which were just a few days away from blooming in vibrant hues. The Dutchman's Breeches, with its white, pants-like blooms, seemed to be scattered everywhere, adding a touch of whimsy to the surroundings. Mia also spotted the elegant Bloodroot, recognized by its single white flower and large leaf, already in full bloom. As she took in the breathtaking scenery, Mia couldn't help but reflect on the beauty of the place. "This is surely God's Heaven on earth!" she thought to herself. "Me-Ma would be in heaven if she could see all of this!" Her eyes then caught sight of the majestic Mountain Laurel, Rhododendron, Sugar Maples, Oaks, and towering Eastern Hemlocks, standing tall and proud. Ferns lined the trail, with the Christmas fern and Lady fern being abundant. In the moist and low areas, Mia spotted the delicate Haircap Moss, adorned with tiny hair-like structures. She couldn't help but feel a sense of wonder at the intricate details of nature. Although it would take a few more weeks for the wild strawberries to bloom, Mia could already see the beginnings of their fruit. The Plums and Blueberries were just putting on their fruit, promising a delightful harvest in the weeks to come. As Mia continued her journey, she couldn't help but feel grateful for the opportunity to immerse herself in such a stunning natural landscape.

Mia, an avid nature lover, embarked on a delightful adventure through a scenic trail with her friends. As they strolled along, Mia couldn't resist the vibrant blooming petals that caught her eye. With a childlike wonder, she carefully plucked several of them and tucked them gently into the pages of her worn-out daily journal. Excitement filled her heart as she jotted down detailed descriptions of each petal and even gave them whimsical names that matched their unique beauty. Despite her fascination with the plant world, Mia often trailed behind the rest of the group. Jake, the experienced hiker, took the lead, confidently navigating the trail they were exploring. Following closely behind Jake were Brian and Roz, who occasionally called out to Mia, urging her to catch up. However, Mia was completely immersed in her own little world, captivated by the enchanting flora that surrounded her. Each step she took was a moment of discovery, a chance to interact with nature in a way that only she could comprehend.

The trail they were embarking on was a challenging one, filled with a variety of obstacles. It was a mixture of rocks, some covered and others uncovered, making every step a potential hazard. The constant maze of tree roots added another layer of complexity to the well-worn path. The narrowness of the trail meant that the four of them had to walk in single file, unable to walk side-by-side. Despite the initial optimism, their goal for the first day was ambitious - they aimed to cover 7.6 miles and reach the Hawk Mountain shelter before setting up camp for the night. Jake, perhaps underestimating the difficulty of the terrain, believed it would be a simple day, especially for the other three. However, as the day wore on, those seven plus miles felt like fifteen to the weary hikers. As they approached the Springer Mountain shelter, they realized their expectations were wrong. The shelter was nothing like they had imagined, merely a lean-to built off the ground. Exhausted and in need of a break, the four of them found solace at the shelter. The girls bonded over their shared struggle with the trail's tough terrain, providing each other with much-needed support and understanding.

As the sun hit midday, Henry Carter, Martha Brown, and James Hilyard from N.C. State in Raleigh approached the shelter. The air was cool, and the quiet sounds of the forest provided a serene backdrop to their conversation. Jake, Mia, Brian, and Roz welcomed them warmly, eager to hear about their journey.

Jake: "Hey there! Looks like you've had quite the hike. Where did you guys start?"

Henry: (smiled wearily.) "Hey! We started near Boone, North Carolina. Seems like ages ago now."

Martha: (nodding) "It's been two weeks on the trail for us. N.C. State has a different spring break schedule than you guys do at Young Harris, I guess."

Brian: "Wow, impressive! You guys must be pros by now."

James: (laughing) "We wish. We're just 2.7 miles away from the end of the trail for us, and let me tell you, we're ready for some civilization."

Mia: "I bet. Two weeks out here must have been tough. You guys look pretty worn out."

Martha: "Yeah, we're weary and totally out of food.

We're so eager to get to the Lodge at Amicalola Falls and have a good, hot meal."

Roz: (empathetically) "I can imagine. It must be rough running out of supplies so close to the end."

Henry: "It is, but we're almost there. Just have to push through a little longer."

Jake: "You guys have done great making it this far. We're planning to head that way, too. Maybe we can stick together for the last stretch?"

James: (gratefully) "That'd be outstanding. Safety in numbers and all that. Plus, it's good to have some company after two weeks of just us three. We met a lot of different folks on the trail, but found not that we could hit it off with."

Brian: "Sorry to hear that, but now you're near the end. Sounds like a splendid plan for dinner. Let's make sure you guys get to that hot meal soon enough."

Mia: "Agreed. And who knows, maybe they'll have some extra desserts for fellow hikers!"

Martha: (smiled.) "That would be amazing right about now."

The group laughed together, their shared experiences and camaraderie creating a bond. As the day wore on, they exchanged stories of their respective journeys, the challenges they faced, and the memories they made. The shelter provided a temporary reprieve as they prepared for the last stretch of their adventure together.

It was time for a much-needed bathroom break, and as Roz and Mia ventured up the hill behind the lean-to, they stumbled upon a rustic, weathered wooden outhouse. Its solitary hole stood as the only option for relieving themselves amidst the wilderness. With a mix of curiosity and trepidation, they cautiously entered the cramped space. The pungent odor overwhelmed their senses, causing them to recoil in surprise. The dilapidated structure and the raw reality of nature's call left a lasting impression on the two adventurers. In that moment, they realized their journey was going to be far more challenging and demanding than they had initially expected.

As the team left the shelter, they met two through-hikers, James and Bill, who had been on the trail from the Georgia border and had spent five days reaching this point, headed to Amicalola. The two men were best friends and hiked a different section each year for a week of together time. Bill was a forty-seven-year-old banker from Atlanta, who had a passion for outdoor adventures. He had always dreamed of conquering the Appalachian Trail, and this year, he finally convinced his friend James to join him. James, a consultant with an engineering firm, was fifty-two and had extensive hiking experience. He often sought solace in nature to escape the demands of his high-pressure job. Both Bill and James were amicable and shared their week-long adventure with the four spring-breakers, eagerly exchanging stories and tips about hiking. James mentioned the group should be on the lookout for black bears, for they had encountered one on Blood Mountain two days prior. He advised the team to remain cautious and take necessary precautions to avoid any potential bear encounters. The spring-breakers nodded, appreciating the valuable advice from the experienced hikers, and continued their journey with a renewed sense of awareness and excitement.

While on their way to Stover Creek Shelter, another two and a half miles from Springer Mountain, Mia, one of the hikers, slipped over one of those trail rocks and gashed her knee. Fortunately, Roz, who was a nurse, could put her nursing skills in use and assist her friend. The hiking group quickly stopped in their tracks, taking off their heavy backpacks, and patiently waited for Roz to work her magic. With a reassuring smile, Roz examined the wound and assured Mia that it was just a minor cut, nothing to be concerned about. She swiftly cleaned the area with a cleansing wipe and applied some Neosporin to prevent any infection. To add a touch of whimsy, Roz even adorned Mia's knee with a cute, little Charlie Brown bandage. The male members of the group couldn't help but snicker when they caught sight of the playful bandage, lightening the mood amid the wilderness.

Everyone enjoyed lunch at the Stover Creek Shelter around 2 p.m. Without starting a campfire, the four took out protein bars and some trail nuts to munch on. Mia's knee was smarting, and she complained about it.

"So," Jake exclaimed. "You don't want to go back to Amicalola, do you?"

"No way, Dude!" Mia shouted enthusiastically. "I'm determined to go all the way. It would be nice to have a little sympathy for a fellow trail mate, though. This Appalachian Trail journey is no walk in the park, after all."

Nestled amongst the tall trees and calming sounds of nature, Jake and Mia contemplated their decision to continue hiking the trail. They had already covered a significant portion of the first day's journey, starting from Amicalola Falls in Georgia. The challenging terrain, unpredictable weather, and physical exertion would soon test their limits, however.

Jake, with his rugged appearance and a determined glint in his eyes, was always up for a challenge. He relished in the thrill of pushing his body to the limit and conquering nature's obstacles. Mia had a more laid-back demeanor but possessed an unwavering resolve. Her love for nature and thirst for adventure fueled her desire to complete the entire trail.

The camaraderie they had developed with their fellow hikers, their shared stories, and the breathtaking views they had witnessed along the way kept their spirits high.

As they sat under the waning afternoon sky, Jake couldn't help but admire Mia's determination. He understood the importance of having a support system on this arduous journey. With a teasing smile, he assured Mia, "Don't worry, I'll always be here to lend a helping hand or a sympathetic ear whenever you need it."

Mia chuckled and playfully nudged Jake. "Thanks, Dude. It's good to know I have someone who understands the struggles and triumphs of this trail. Together, we'll conquer every mile and create memories that will last a lifetime." Little did Mia know what was ahead of them. Life can turn on a dime. Suddenly, what would seem to be a wonderful journey could turn disastrous and cruel.

With that, Mia takes off down the hillside for a potty break and headed into the woods, the sounds of nature surrounding her.

Finding a secluded spot, she settled in when she heard a rustling noise nearby. Her heart skipped a beat as she turned her head slowly, her eyes widening in shock. Just a few yards away, a female black bear emerged from the underbrush, her cub trailing closely behind.

Mia froze, her breath catching in her throat. The bear's dark eyes locked onto hers, and for a moment, time seemed to stand still. She knew black bears were not aggressive, but a mother bear with a cub could be unpredictable and protective.

Keeping as still as possible, Mia remembered the advice she had read about bear encounters. She avoided direct eye contact, trying to appear non-threatening. The bear sniffed the air, assessing the situation, while the cub playfully pawed at the ground.

Mia's mind raced, but she remained calm, slowly and quietly reaching for the bear spray clipped to her belt. She knew sudden movements could provoke the bear, so she moved with deliberate caution. The mother bear, satisfied that Mia posed no immediate threat, nudged her cub away, heading back into the forest.

As the bears disappeared into the trees, Mia let out a shaky breath, her heart still pounding. She quickly finished her business and hurried back to the campsite, her encounter with the wild leaving her both shaken and in awe of the majestic creatures she had just witnessed.

Mia quickly returned to camp and shared her experience with the team. "I was so afraid," Mia said. "I've seen nothing like that before and feared for my life. Now that it's over, I feel blessed to have escaped alive."

Jake, with his trail wisdom, said, "Folks, I remind you again about the dangers of the trail. You MUST be careful and look around yourself constantly."

With renewed determination and a shared sense of adventure, Jake, Mia, Brian and Roz embraced the challenges that lay ahead. The Appalachian Trail beckoned, promising breathtaking vistas, unforgettable encounters, and the ultimate test of their strength and perseverance.

To reach the Gooch Gap Shelter, the team, at their pace, needed to hike for another three to four hours. They continued at a steady pace, their laughter and jokes punctuated by shared life stories.

About an hour later, Brian asked Jake to take a break while he took care of some business down the hill, so the team took off their backpacks and sat on some large boulders, awaiting Brian's return.

While the rest of the group tended to their camp chores, Brian explored a narrow side trail he had noticed earlier. The sun was still high, casting dappled patterns of light through the dense canopy above. The beckoning trail seemed like an invitation to a hidden world waiting to be discovered.

Brian's boots crunched softly on the leaf-strewn path as he ventured further into the forest. The air was cooler here, filled with the scent of earth and pine. After a short hike, he heard the gentle babbling of a stream nearby. Drawn by the sound, he pushed through a cluster of ferns and stood by a crystal-clear brook.

As he crouched down to cup the cool water in his hands, movement in the corner of his eye caught his attention. Slowly, he looked up to see a magnificent sight—a herd of deer gracefully moving through the trees. There were about ten of them, their coats a rich brown, blending seamlessly with the surrounding forest. Some of the younger deer pranced playfully, while the older ones moved with a deliberate elegance.

Brian watched in awe, careful not to make any sudden movements that might startle the herd. He could see a few of them drinking from the stream, their ears twitching at the slightest sound. The scene was serene, almost magical, as if time had slowed down just for this moment.

The lead doe lifted her head, her large, dark eyes meeting Brian's. There was a sense of mutual respect in their silent exchange, a recognition of the shared space between human and wildlife. The herd moved gracefully, disappearing into the deeper woods, leaving Brian with a sense of profound peace and connection.

He stayed by the stream for a while longer, soaking in the tranquility before he reluctantly headed back to the campsite. The sight of the deer lingered in his mind, a gentle reminder of the beauty and stillness that nature offered amidst the challenges of their journey.

As Brian made his way back to camp, his steps light after witnessing the serene beauty of the deer herd, the forest transitioned into twilight. The soft glow of the sun filtered through the foliage, casting long shadows across the path. The air was still, save for the occasional rustle of leaves and distant bird calls.

Suddenly, a rustling sound ahead caught his attention. He paused, squinting through the dimming light, and saw a sleek, tawny coyote slipping silently through the under-brush. The animal paused in the middle of the trail, its keen eyes catching Brian's.

For a moment, Brian stood still, holding his breath. The coyote's presence was both surprising and mesmer-izing. Its fur blended perfectly with the autumnal hues of the forest floor, making it appear almost ghost-like in the dusk. The coyote, aware but indifferent to Brian's pres-ence, seemed at ease, exuding a quiet confidence.

The two shared a brief, silent connection—a testament to the untamed and mysterious rhythm of the wilderness. Then, with a last glance, the coyote continued its way, disappearing into the shadows as swiftly and silently as it had appeared.

Brian let out the breath he had been holding and continued his trek back to camp, his heart still racing from the encounter. The sight of the coyote, coupled with the earlier deer herd, reinforced the raw beauty of the Appalachian Trail and the wild surprises it held.

His mind buzzed with excitement as he approached the camp, ready to share his unexpected wildlife sightings with his friends. As he arrived, the warmth of the campfire and the familiar faces of his companions greeted him, adding a sense of camaraderie to his newfound tales of the wild.

Brian's face was lit up with excitement at witnessing the herd of deer and the coyote crossing his path. The group gathered around to hear about the adventure of his adventure.

Jake: (curious) "Hey, Brian! You look like you've seen a ghost. What happened out there?"

Brian: (grinning) "You won't believe it! I wandered off down that side trail towards a stream and, guess what? I saw an entire herd of deer!"

Mia: (excitedly) "No way! How many were there?"

Brian: (counting on his fingers) "About ten! They were just grazing and moving so gracefully. It was like something out of a nature documentary."

Roz: (smiled) "That sounds magical. Did they notice you?"

Brian: "Yeah, the lead doe actually looked right at me. It was like we had this moment... Mutual respect, you know?"

Jake: "That's amazing, Brian. But you look more excited than just a deer sighting. What else happened?"

Brian: (eyes wide) "On my way back, I saw a coyote! It crossed the path right ahead of me. Almost felt like it was checking me out."

Mia: (widening her eyes) "A coyote? You're like a wildlife magnet today!"

Brian: "I know, right? It was surreal. The coyote just glanced at me and then disappeared into the trees. I felt like I was part of the wild for a moment."

Roz: "Encounters like that are rare. Looks like the trail wanted to treat you to some wildlife magic today."

Jake: (laughing) "Well, next time you wander off, take a camera! We want evidence of your wildlife adventures."

Brian: (still buzzing) "I'll capture it next time. It was just incredible. Reminded me why we're out here—to connect with nature in its purest form."

The group shared in Brian's excitement, their bond strengthened by the shared experiences and natural wonders of the Appalachian Trail. They settled back onto the trail, feeling inspired and grateful for the adventure they were on.

Undeterred, we made our way through the check-in point and immediately began ascending a steep paved road that led to the Amicalola Lodge. Perched atop the mountain overlooking the magnificent falls, the lodge offered breathtaking views and a sense of serenity. Among our group, Jake and Mia were the only ones who had visited the park before, giving them a sense of familiarity and confidence in navigating the area. In fact, Jake had even arranged with the Park officials to leave his truck in one of the Lodge's parking spaces for the duration of our two-week hike. While Jake went inside to complete the arrangements with the lodge staff, the rest eagerly unloaded their gear and began preparing themselves for the adventure that awaited.

Jake, a seasoned hiker, soon returned to the group and eagerly grabbed his gear, which comprised a sturdy backpack, a comfortable sleeping bag, and essential camping supplies. As they gathered at the trailhead, the group formed a circle, creating a sense of unity and anticipation. Brian, a devout believer, took on the role of spiritual leader and offered a heartfelt prayer for God's protection throughout their journey. With humble words, he implored, "Dear God, we humbly ask for your blessings and guidance as we embark on this incredible adventure. May your presence always be with us, providing us with

strength, wisdom, and protection. We pray for joy and
excitement on this journey, allowing us to fully experience
the wonders of your creation. As we dedicate ourselves to
you, may we fulfill your divine will in our lives. Amen."

The four friends made their way to the trailhead. The
scent of fresh pine and the sounds of birds chirping filled
the air as they took their first steps onto the Appalachian Trail. Ahead of them lay countless miles of untamed
wilderness, challenging ascents, and breathtaking vistas.
They were ready to embrace the adventure and create
memories that would last a lifetime.

As they headed up the 2.8-mile trek to Springer Mountain, the air was brisk and cool. The young adults had
prepared well, however, and had packed the necessary
clothing for the journey. Mia, the would-be horticulturist, found the abundance of plant species along the trail
captivating. She marveled at the Spring Beauty, one of
the earliest bloomers, with its petite flowers and delicate
pink and white petals. Mia observed that these beautiful
flowers mostly thrived in the low, moist, wooded areas
of the trail. As she continued, she could not help but
notice the promising growth of Fire Pinks and Flame
Azaleas, which were just a few days away from blooming in vibrant hues. The Dutchman's Breeches, with its
white, pants-like blooms, seemed to be scattered every-

where, adding a touch of whimsy to the surroundings. Mia also spotted the elegant Bloodroot, recognized by its single white flower and large leaf, already in full bloom. As she took in the breathtaking scenery, Mia could not help but reflect on the beauty of the place. "This is surely God's Heaven on earth!" she thought to herself. Her eyes then caught sight of the majestic Mountain Laurel, Rhododendron, Sugar Maples, Oaks, and towering Eastern Hemlocks, standing tall and proud. Ferns lined the trail, with the Christmas fern and Lady fern being abundant. In the moist and low areas, Mia spotted the delicate Haircap Moss, adorned with tiny hair-like structures. She could not help but feel a sense of wonder at the intricate details of nature. Although it would take a few more weeks for the wild strawberries to bloom, Mia could already see the beginnings of their fruit. The Plums and Blueberries were just putting on their fruit, promising a delightful harvest in the weeks to come. As Mia continued her journey, she could not help but feel grateful for the opportunity to immerse herself in such a stunning natural landscape.

Mia, an avid nature lover, embarked on a delightful adventure through a scenic trail with her friends. As they strolled along, Mia could not resist the vibrant blooming petals that caught her eye. With a childlike wonder, she carefully plucked several of them and tucked them gently into the pages of her worn-out daily journal. Excitement filled her heart as she jotted down detailed descriptions of each petal and even gave them whimsical names that matched their unique beauty. Despite her fascination with the plant world, Mia often trailed behind the rest of the group. Jake, the experienced hiker, took the lead, confidently navigating the trail they were exploring. Following closely behind Jake were Brian and Roz, who occasionally called out to Mia, urging her to catch up. However, Mia was completely immersed in her own little world, captivated by the enchanting flora that surrounded her. Each step she took was a moment of discovery, a chance to interact with nature in a way that only she could comprehend.

The trail they were embarking on was a challenging one, filled with a variety of obstacles. It was a mixture of rocks, some covered and others uncovered, making every step a potential hazard. The constant maze of tree roots added another layer of complexity to the well-worn path. The narrowness of the trail meant that the four of them had to walk in single file, unable to walk side-by-side. Despite the initial optimism, their goal for the first day was ambitious - they aimed to cover 7.6 miles and reach the Hawk Mountain shelter before setting up camp for the night. Jake, underestimating the difficulty of the terrain, believed it would be a simple day, especially for the other three. However, as the day wore on, those seven plus miles felt like fifteen to the weary hikers. As they approached the Springer Mountain shelter, they realized their expectations were wrong. The shelter was nothing like they had imagined, merely lean-tos built off the ground. Exhausted and in need of a break, the four of them found solace at the shelter. The girls bonded over their shared struggle with the trail's tough terrain, providing each other with much-needed support and understanding.

It was time for a much-needed bathroom break, and as Roz and Mia ventured up the hill behind the lean-to, they stumbled upon a rustic, weathered wooden outhouse. Its solitary hole stood as the only option for relieving themselves amidst the wilderness. With a mix of curiosity and trepidation, they cautiously entered the cramped space. The pungent odor overwhelmed their senses, causing them to recoil in surprise. The dilapidated structure and the raw reality of nature's call left an impression on the two adventurers. In that moment, they realized their journey was going to be far more challenging and demanding than they had initially expected.

As the team left the shelter, they met two through-hikers, James and Bill, who had been on the trail from the Georgia border and had spent five days reaching this point, headed to Amicalola. The two men were best friends and hiked a different section each year for a week of together time. Bill was a forty-seven-year-old banker from Atlanta, who had a passion for outdoor adventures. He had always dreamed of conquering the Appalachian Trail, and this year, he finally convinced his friend James to join him. James, a consultant with an engineering firm, was fifty-two and had extensive hiking experience. He often sought solace in nature to escape the demands of his high-pressure job. Both Bill and James were amicable and shared their week-long adventure with the four spring-breakers, eagerly exchanging stories and tips about hiking. James mentioned the group should be on the lookout for black bears, for they had encountered one on Blood Mountain two days prior. He advised the team to remain cautious and take necessary precautions to avoid any potential bear encounters. The spring-breakers nodded, appreciating the valuable advice from the experienced hikers, and continued their journey with a renewed sense of awareness and excitement.

While on their way to Stover Creek Shelter, another two and a half miles from Springer Mountain, Mia, one of the hikers, slipped over one of those trail rocks and gashed her knee. Fortunately, Roz, who was a nurse, could put her nursing skills in use and assist her friend. The hiking group suddenly stopped in their tracks, taking off their heavy backpacks, and patiently waited for Roz to work her magic. With a reassuring smile, Roz examined the wound and assured Mia that it was just a minor cut, nothing to be concerned about. She swiftly cleaned the area with a cleansing wipe and applied some Neosporin to prevent any infection. To add a touch of whimsy, Roz even adorned Mia's knee with a cute, little Charlie Brown bandage. The male members of the group could not help but snicker when they caught sight of the playful bandage, lightening the mood amid the wilderness.

Everyone enjoyed lunch at the Stover Creek Shelter around 2 p.m. Without starting a campfire, the four took out protein bars and some trail nuts to munch on. Mia's knee was smarting, and she complained about it.

"So," Jake exclaimed. "You don't want to go back to Amicalola, do you?"

"No way, Dude!" Mia shouted enthusiastically. "I'm determined to go all the way. It would be nice to have a little sympathy for a fellow trail mate, though. This Appalachian Trail journey is no walk in the park, after all."

As they sat there on the side of the trail, surrounded by towering trees and the soothing sounds of nature, Jake and Mia contemplated their decision to continue hiking the Appalachian Trail. They had already covered a sizable portion of the first day's journey, starting from Amicalola

Falls in Georgia. The challenging terrain, unpredictable weather, and physical exertion would soon test their limits, however.

Jake, with his rugged appearance and a determined glint in his eyes, was always up for a challenge. He relished in the thrill of pushing his body to the limit and conquering nature's obstacles. Mia had a more laid-back demeanor but possessed an unwavering resolve. Her love for nature and thirst for adventure fueled her desire to complete the entire trail.

The camaraderie they had developed with their fellow hikers, their shared stories, and the breathtaking views they had witnessed along the way kept their spirits high.

As they sat under the waning afternoon sky, Jake could not help but admire Mia's determination. He understood the importance of having a support system on this arduous journey. With a teasing smile, he assured Mia, "Don't worry, I'll always be here to lend a helping hand or a sympathetic ear whenever you need it."

Mia chuckled and playfully nudged Jake. "Thanks, Dude. It's good to know I have someone who understands the struggles and triumphs of this trail. Together, we'll conquer every mile and create memories that will last a lifetime." Little did Mia know what was ahead of them. Life can turn on a dime. Suddenly, what would seem to be a wonderful journey could turn disastrous and cruel.

With that, Mia takes off down the hillside for a potty break and headed into the woods, the sounds of nature surrounding her.

Finding a secluded spot, she settled in when she heard a rustling noise nearby. Her heart skipped a beat as she turned her head slowly, her eyes widening in shock. Just a few yards away, a female black bear emerged from the underbrush, her cub trailing closely behind.

Mia froze, her breath catching in her throat. The bear's dark eyes locked onto hers, and for a moment, time seemed to stand still. She knew black bears were not aggressive, but a mother bear with a cub could be unpredictable and protective.

Keeping as still as possible, Mia remembered the advice she had read about bear encounters. She avoided direct eye contact, trying to appear non-threatening. The bear sniffed the air, assessing the situation, while the cub playfully pawed at the ground.

Mia's mind raced, but she remained calm, slowly and quietly reaching for the bear spray clipped to her belt. She knew sudden movements could provoke the bear, so she moved with deliberate caution. The mother bear, satisfied that Mia posed no immediate threat, nudged her cub away, heading back into the forest.

As the bears disappeared into the trees, Mia let out a shaky breath, her heart still pounding. She quickly finished her business and hurried back to the campsite, her encounter with the wild leaving her both shaken and in awe of the majestic creatures she had just witnessed.

Mia quickly returned to camp and shared her experience with the team. "I was so afraid," Mia said. "I've seen nothing like that before and feared for my life. Now that it's over, I feel blessed to have escaped alive."

Jake, with his trail wisdom, said, "Folks, I remind you again about the dangers of the trail. You MUST be careful and look around yourself constantly."

With renewed determination and a shared sense of adventure, Jake, Mia, Brian and Roz embraced the challenges that lay ahead. The Appalachian Trail beckoned, promising breathtaking vistas, unforgettable encounters, and the ultimate test of their strength and perseverance.

To reach the Gooch Gap Shelter, the team, at their pace, needed to hike for another three to four hours. They continued at a steady pace, their laughter and jokes punctuated by shared life stories.

About an hour later, Brian asked Jake to take a break while he took care of some business down the hill, so the team took off their backpacks and sat on some large boulders, awaiting Brian's return.

While the rest of the group tended to their camp chores, Brian explored a narrow side trail he had noticed earlier. The sun was still high, casting dappled patterns of light through the dense canopy above. The beckoning trail seemed like an invitation to a hidden world waiting to be discovered.

Brian's boots crunched softly on the leaf-strewn path as he ventured further into the forest. The air was cooler here, filled with the scent of earth and pine. After a short hike, he heard the gentle babbling of a stream nearby. Drawn by the sound, he pushed through a cluster of ferns and stood by a clear brook.

As he crouched down to cup the cool water in his hands, movement in the corner of his eye caught his attention. Slowly, he looked up to see a magnificent sight—a herd of deer gracefully moving through the trees. There were about ten of them, their coats a rich brown, blending seamlessly with the surrounding forest. Some of the younger deer pranced playfully, while the older ones moved with a deliberate elegance.

Brian watched in awe, careful not to make any sudden movements that might startle the herd. He could see a few of them drinking from the stream, their ears twitching at the slightest sound. The scene was serene, almost magical, as if time had slowed down just for this moment.

The lead doe lifted her head, her large, dark eyes meeting Brian's. There was a sense of mutual respect in their silent exchange, a recognition of the shared space between human and wildlife. The herd moved gracefully, disappearing into the deeper woods, leaving Brian with a sense of profound peace and connection.

He stayed by the stream for a while longer, soaking in the tranquility before he reluctantly headed back to the campsite. The sight of the deer lingered in his mind, a gentle reminder of the beauty and stillness that nature offered amidst the challenges of their journey.

As Brian made his way back to camp, his steps light after witnessing the serene beauty of the deer herd, the forest transitioned into twilight. The soft glow of the sun filtered through the foliage, casting long shadows across the path. The air was still, save for the occasional rustle of leaves and distant bird calls.

Suddenly, a rustling sound ahead caught his attention. He paused, squinting through the dimming light, and saw a sleek, tawny coyote slipping silently through the underbrush. The animal paused in the middle of the trail, its keen eyes catching Brian's.

For a moment, Brian stood still, holding his breath. The coyote's presence was both surprising and mesmerizing. Its fur blended perfectly with the autumnal hues of the forest floor, making it appear ghost-like in the dusk. The coyote, aware but indifferent to Brian's presence, seemed at ease, exuding a quiet confidence.

The two shared a brief, silent connection—a testament to the untamed and mysterious rhythm of the wilderness. Then, with a last glance, the coyote continued its way, disappearing into the shadows as swiftly and silently as it had appeared.

Brian let out the breath he had been holding and continued his trek back to camp, his heart still racing from the encounter. The sight of the coyote, coupled with the earlier deer herd, reinforced the raw beauty of the Appalachian Trail and the wild surprises it held.

His mind buzzed with excitement as he approached the camp, ready to share his unexpected wildlife sightings with his friends. As he arrived, the warmth of the campfire and the familiar faces of his companions greeted him, adding a sense of camaraderie to his newfound tales of the wild.

Brian's face was lit up with excitement at witnessing the herd of deer and the coyote crossing his path. The group gathered around to hear about the adventure of his adventure.

Jake: (curious) "Hey, Brian! You look like you've seen a ghost. What happened out there?"

Brian: (grinning) "You won't believe it! I wandered off

down that side trail towards a stream and, guess what? I saw an entire herd of deer!"

Mia: (excitedly) "No way! How many were there?"

Brian: (counting on his fingers) "About ten! They were just grazing and moving so gracefully. It was like something out of a nature documentary."

Roz: (smiled) "That sounds magical. Did they notice you?"

Brian: "Yeah, the lead doe actually looked right at me. It was like we had this moment... Mutual respect, you know?"

Jake: "That's amazing, Brian. But you look more excited than just a deer sighting. What else happened?"

Brian: (eyes wide) "On my way back, I saw a coyote! It crossed the path right ahead of me. Almost felt like it was checking me out."

Mia: (widening her eyes) "A coyote? You're like a wildlife magnet today!"

Brian: "I know, right? It was surreal. The coyote just glanced at me and then disappeared into the trees. I felt like I was part of the wild for a moment."

Roz: "Encounters like that are rare. Looks like the trail wanted to treat you to some wildlife magic today."

Jake: (laughing) "Well, next time you wander off, take a camera! We want evidence of your wildlife adventures."

Brian: (still buzzing) "I'll capture it next time. It was just incredible. Reminded me why we're out here—to connect with nature in its purest form."

The group shared in Brian's excitement, their bond strengthened by the shared experiences and natural wonders of the Appalachian Trail. They settled back onto the trail, feeling inspired and grateful for the adventure they were on.

5

Gooch Gap

Wearily, after a long day of hiking, the team arrived at the Gooch Gap Shelter, a popular resting spot for through-hikers on the trail. Exhausted and hoping for a bit of solitude, they were disappointed to find the shelter already filled with at least ten other backpackers. Determined to find their own space, the team hiked a little further to a small clearing down the hill and across a Georgia Power service road to set up camp.

Jake: "We have little time left; therefore, we must hurry."

Brian: "What do you want me to do, Jake?"

Jake: "Let's get our tent set up first, Brian, and then we can help the ladies."

Brian: "Sounds like a plan, Jake. Let's get to it."

Setting up camp proved to be a challenge, especially for the girls, Roz and Mia, who were using their tents for the first time. With the patient help of the guys, they figured out the intricacies of tent assembly and finally got their shelters ready. As they worked, the distant rumble of thunder served as a reminder of the unpredictable nature of the night ahead.

Once the tents were up, the team turned their attention to building a fire. Brian and Jake, resourceful and experienced hikers, gathered rocks from the surrounding area to outline the fire pit. They also gathered enough wood to sustain them through the chilly night ahead. As they carefully arranged the wood and ignited the flames, the crackling fire warmed their tired bodies and lifted their spirits.

As darkness enveloped the forest and the distant thunder grew louder, the team couldn't help but feel a sense of trepidation. The ominous atmosphere painted a picture of a potentially stormy and restless night. However, they were grateful for the shelter of their tents and the comforting glow of the fire, providing a sense of security in the wilderness. The night ahead would prove again to be challenging and would test their perseverance.

With their water canteens near empty, Roz and Jake knew they needed to find a water source soon. They hiked down a little trail that they had spotted earlier, hoping it would lead them to a brook or stream. After a few minutes of walking, they stumbled upon a beautiful little brook nestled between the trees. The sound of the flowing water was like music to their ears. They quickly took out their water filtration system and began filtering the water. Each canteen took a few minutes to fill, but the wait was worth it. As they watched the clear water flow into their canteens, a sense of relief washed over them. They knew that once they had replenished their water supplies, they could continue their hike with renewed energy and hydration.

Back at camp, each prepared their dinner and enjoyed a time of camaraderie and sharing.

The four friends settled around the campfire, their dinners steaming in the cool evening air. The storm had moved on, but distant rumbles of thunder echoed through the mountains, adding a dramatic backdrop to their conversations.

Jake: (taking a bite) "So, what's the highlight of everyone's day?"

Brian: (smiled) "The deer, without a doubt. Watching them move so gracefully was mesmerizing. And that coyote crossing the path was the icing on the cake."

Mia: (nodding) "I can't believe you saw that! Makes my favorite moment seem mundane by comparison."

Roz: (grinning) "Come on, Mia. Share yours."

Mia: (thoughtfully) "Alright, alright. I loved the close encounter with the mother bear and her cub. I felt at one with the forest and nature."

Jake: (chuckling) "Brian's magical wildlife encounters and Mia's enchanted forest. We're living in a storybook, folks."

Roz: (smiled) "It feels like it, doesn't it? Being out here is a reminder of how connected we are to nature. The brewing storm may test us, but we will face whatever comes together."

Brian: (raising his cup) "To surviving the storm and more adventures to come. We've got each other, and that's what matters."

Jake: (lifting his cup) "Hear, hear! To many more tales of the trail."

As they clinked their cups together, the distant thunder continued its gentle reminder of nature's power. The fire crackled, casting a warm light on their faces as they shared stories and laughter, each tale weaving them tighter into the fabric of their journey.

Roz: (smiled) "Remember that time we got lost and ended up finding that hidden waterfall? That was a blessing in disguise."

Mia: (laughing) "Yeah, who knew getting lost could lead to something so beautiful? This trail has a way of surprising us."

Roz: (reflectively) "It teaches us resilience and gratitude.

Every challenge, every beautiful moment—it's all part of the adventure."

Brian: (grinning) "And we've got plenty more miles to cover. To the trail ahead and the stories we'll create."

The fire flickered, and the night wore on, their laughter and stories mingling with the sounds of the wilderness. Together, they faced whatever came their way, knowing that each step brought them closer to new experiences and deeper bonds.

No one mentioned being tired or wanting to go home. The team of four backpackers was a solid team. They had spent two days on the trail and were expecting many more adventures along the way.

The group had settled in at Gooch Gap, their muscles sore but spirits high from the day's trek. As night fell, the air grew thick with humidity, an ominous heaviness pressing down on them. They tried to sleep, but a sense of unease tingled at the edge of their consciousness.

By midnight, the distant rumble of thunder grew louder. Dark clouds gathered overhead, gnashing together in a display of nature's fury. The first flash of lightning lit up the tents, casting sharp, eerie shadows.

At around 1 a.m., the storm hit with full force. The sky cracked open as blinding lightning bolts split the heavens, illuminating the shelter in harsh, brief bursts. The deafening roar of thunder followed, rolling through the mountains like a furious beast. Rain poured down in relentless sheets, hammering the roof of the tents with a ferocity that drowned out all other sounds.

Inside, the hikers huddled together, their hearts pounding. The storm's wrath was unrelenting, and soon, water began seeping into the tents, pooling on the floor and soaking their gear. They lit their lanterns, casting a flickering light on faces taut with fear and determination.

As the minutes dragged into agonizing hours, the rain intensified, and what had started as a mere inconvenience turned into a terrifying ordeal. Quickly turning to mud, rivers of water streaming down the slopes threatened the ground outside, threatening to flood their refuge. The hikers scrambled to secure their belongings, trying to keep dry anything they could.

Desperation filled the air as the tents creaked and strained against the onslaught. Each clap of thunder elicited gasps and reflexive movements; their nerves frayed by the unending barrage. Water levels rose, and the realization hit: they were at the mercy of the storm.

Wading through the ankle-deep water, they repositioned themselves, trying to find higher ground within the limited space. Sleep was impossible, replaced by an anxious vigil as they watched the storm rage on. The long night stretched endlessly, with each minute feeling like an eternity.

Finally, as dawn approached, the storm abated. The rain lessened, and the once-violent thunder now rumbled softly in the distance. Exhausted but relieved, the hikers surveyed the damage. Their gear soaked, and their bodies weary, they had survived.

The storm had tested their resolve, and as the first light of morning crept over the horizon, they felt a renewed sense of camaraderie and resilience. They shared tired smiles and words of encouragement, knowing they had faced nature's fury and emerged stronger.

As Jake fought feverishly to create a firm, it was futile.

Jake worriedly stated, "We must go to the shelter and confirm the campers' departure. If they are, then we will camp out in the shelter for the day and again try out all of our gear."

Roz: "What if they're still there? What will we do then?"

Brian said, with a light heart, "Roz, looks like we'll continue our hike with damp gear."

Roz: (disgusted) "Those are not nice things to say. That's not like you at all."

Brian: (apologetically) "Roz, please forgive me if I upset you. It felt like the night would never end. We're all weary and fidgety. We should rest before continuing."

Mia compassionately said, "Guys, we love each other, and we know God is with us. I'm going to pray that the shelter is empty. Let's have faith that it is."

And sure enough, when the team arrived at the shelter, they found it empty, showing that the folks they were expecting had already departed. It seemed likely that they had headed south on the trail, in pursuit of their adventure. Eager to replenish their energy and rejuvenate their spirits, the team took advantage of the vacant shelter. They settled in, resting and drying out their damp clothing. They artfully suspended sleeping bags from sturdy tree limbs and draped them across the top of the shelter, creating a makeshift clothesline. Jake, demonstrating his resourcefulness and preparedness as a true Boy Scout, skillfully started a fire using firebugs he had ingeniously crafted back at home. The crackling flames provided a much-needed warmth, enveloping the weary bodies of the team members and bringing a sense of comfort to their tired souls. Grateful for the foresight to pack their clothes in waterproof bags, the team was relieved to discover that their garments remained dry inside their backpacks. This stroke of luck allowed them to retrieve their warm clothing and dress in layers, ensuring adequate protection against the chilly morning air.

Within a few minutes, a young couple came down the trail and stopped at the shelter and asked if they could warm by the fire. Dan and Jenny were from Sarasota, Florida, and were also on spring break. They planned to go to Unicoi Gap, where friends would pick them up for their trip home. They were such a lovely couple and seemed to be in great shape.

Last evening's storm dominated their team discussions. Showing empathy, the team shared their breakfasts with the couple.

Dan studied at Florida Atlantic University, while Jenny worked as a registered nurse in Boca Raton. Sharing the Christian faith, they deeply loved and cared for Roz, Brian, Jake, and Mia. Following a heartfelt prayer, the couple bid the four farewells, offering strength for their journey, before heading north.

Morning cast a warm glow over Gooch Gap Shelter. The rain had subsided, leaving behind a misty, calm stillness. The hikers, exhausted from the storm, began their routine of drying out their equipment.

"That was an unbelievably wild storm!" exclaimed Jake, wringing out his soaked sleeping bag. It was unlike anything I had ever witnessed.

Roz, nodding as she laid out her gear to dry, replied, "It was intense. I'm just glad we all stayed safe. We must dry this stuff to prevent mold."

Mia: (sipping a cup of lukewarm coffee) "Guess they don't catch everything. Any chance we can catch a break? I must've checked the weather app a dozen times."

Brian: (stretching, looking at the clear sky) "It looks like we might. The sun's strong today, should help dry everything out fast."

As they set up a makeshift drying line and hung their damp clothes and sleeping bags, the group shared stories of their midnight adventure, laughter mixing with the relief of surviving the storm.

Mia: (grinning) "I can't believe we were basically swimming in our shelter last night. It was like Mother Nature gave us a challenge."

Roz: (smirking) "Challenge accepted and conquered. Though, can't say I enjoyed the part where our food almost floated away."

Brian: (jokingly) "Hey, at least if it had, we'd have our first-ever underwater picnic. Gourmet camping at its finest."

Jake: (laughing) "Just another day in the life of Appalachian adventurers. We'll have quite the story to tell once we get back."

As the day wore on, the hikers took turns napping, their bodies still recovering from the night's ordeal. The sound of gear rustling and light-hearted banter created a comfortable atmosphere.

Roz: (lying down, eyes half-closed) "So what's the plan after everything's dry? Push on forward or take another rest day?"

Jake: (reflectively) "Depends on how we feel tomorrow, I think. No rush to move out if we're not ready. Safety first."

Mia: (murmuring) "Agreed. Let's see how we feel after a good night's sleep. No more mid-storm adventures tonight, please."

The group continued their day, balancing rest with prepping their gear, until the sun began its descent again. The memory of the storm lingered, but so did a newfound sense of camaraderie and resilience.

As the group settled into their routine at camp, Jake felt the familiar call of exploration tugging at him. He took a solitary hike up a side trail that wound its way up the mountain. A narrow, less-traveled path promised the thrill of the unknown.

The surrounding forest grew denser as he ascended, the canopy closing overhead. The air was cooler, filled with the earthy scent of moss and pine. Jake's heart raced with excitement as he pushed further along the trail, eager to see what lay ahead.

After an hour of steady hiking, he reached a steep incline. The trail became rocky, and he had to use his hands to steady himself as he climbed. The sound of a rushing waterfall caught his attention, drawing him toward a hidden cascade.

Jake rounded a bend and found himself on a precarious cliff side, with the trail narrowing dangerously. Loose rocks made the footing uncertain, but the view of the waterfall was breathtaking. He took a moment to catch his breath and admire the sight.

Suddenly, a loud crack echoed off the cliffs, and the ground beneath Jake shifted. A section of the trail gave way, sending him scrambling for a foothold. He slid several feet down the rocky slope, his heart pounding as he fought to regain his balance.

Jake: (struggling) "Whoa! That was close. I need to be more careful."

Finding a stable ledge, Jake took a breath, calming his nerves. But his relief was short-lived. He noticed a large boulder above him, dislodged by his slip, teetering precariously. It could come crashing down at any moment.

Jake: (thinking quickly) "I've got to move fast."

With adrenaline coursing through his veins, Jake scanned his surroundings. To his left, a narrow ledge offered an escape route. He carefully maneuvered, inching his way over the treacherous ground, trying not to disturb the unstable rocks.

Just as he reached the ledge, the boulder above shifted again. Jake held his breath, pressing himself against the cliff as the massive rock tumbled down, crashing into the path where he had been moments before.

Jake: (breathless) "That was way too close. Time to head back."

Jake carefully traced his steps back down the trail, each move deliberate and cautious. His mind raced with the realization of how close he had come to serious injury—or worse. The thrill of the adventure had taken a perilous turn, and he knew he needed to rejoin his friends.

Returning to camp, Jake found the group huddled around the fire, their faces lighting up as he approached.

Brian: (concerned) "Jake! You, okay? You look like you've just seen a ghost."

Mia: (worried) "What happened out there?"

Jake: (shaken but smiled) "Just had a bit of a scare. Almost got caught under a falling boulder. It reminded me that this trail's beauty comes with its own dangers."

Roz: (seriously) "Glad you made it back safely. It's a friendly reminder for all of us to be cautious out here."

Jake: (nodding) "Absolutely. Every step out here is an adventure, but we need to stay vigilant. Nature isn't always forgiving."

The group shared a moment of gratitude, their bond strengthened by Jake's close call. They knew that while the Appalachian Trail offered incredible beauty and awe-inspiring moments, it also demanded respect and caution.

As the evening progressed, the group settled into their routines at the Gooch Gap Shelter. Mia, feeling restless, took a short stroll behind the shelter, seeking a moment of quiet amidst nature. The air was cool, and the wind gently rustled the leaves, creating a soothing backdrop to the stillness.

Mia wandered further into the trees, her steps light and careful. She took a deep breath, savoring the fresh, earthy scent of the forest. Suddenly, she paused, her ears catching a faint sound amidst the whispers of the wind. It was subtle at first, almost drowned out by the rustling leaves, but then it grew clearer—voices, faint and incoherent, carried by the breeze.

Her heart quickened, a mix of curiosity and unease washing over her. She scanned the area, trying to pinpoint the source of the voices. The wind seemed to play tricks on her, making it difficult to discern whether the voices were real or just her imagination.

Mia: (murmuring to herself) "Am I hearing things, or is someone really out there?"

She stood still; the voices drifting in and out with the gusts of wind. They were indistinct, like whispers echoing through the forest. Mia strained to catch any recognizable words, but they remained elusive. An eerie melody carried on the air.

Mia: (whispering) "This is so strange... Should I check it out, or head back?"

The sense of mystery deepened as the voices continued, a haunting lullaby mingling with the natural sounds of the woods. Mia's pulse raced, her mind torn between exploring further and returning to the safety of the shelter. The wind's chill seemed to bite a little harder as she deliberated on her next move.

Realizing the potential danger of venturing too far alone, Mia headed back to the shelter. She walked briskly, casting occasional glances over her shoulder, the uncanny experience leaving her unsettled. As she rejoined the group by the campfire, she couldn't shake the feeling of being watched, the whispered voices still echoing in her ears.

Jake: (noticing her expression) "Everything okay, Mia? You look a bit spooked."

Mia: (hesitant) "I'm not sure. I just heard some strange voices while I was out there. It sounded like people, but I couldn't make out any words."

Brian: (frowning) "Voices? Are you sure it wasn't just

the wind playing tricks?"

Mia: (shaking her head) "Maybe, but it felt different. Almost like whispers... It was eerie."

Roz: (concerned) "We should stay together. Let's not take any risks, especially after everything we've been through."

The group fell quiet for a moment, the sound of the wind mingling with the crackling fire. The night felt a little less secure, the forest's mysteries lingering around the edges of their camp.

As the sun dipped below the horizon, casting a twilight glow over the Appalachian Trail, Jake, Mia, Brian, and Josie settled into their camp. The air was cool, and the rhythmic clapping of the water from the river down below the camp created a soothing backdrop for their conversations.

They gathered around the campfire, their faces illuminated by the flickering flames. The distant rumble of thunder still echoed through the mountains, adding a touch of suspense to the night.

Jake: (reminiscing) "Remember that storm back last night? We've come a long way since then."

Brian: (nodding) "Yeah, and it's strengthened us. We've had our fair share of challenges, but nothing can beat our resolve."

Mia: (pensively) "There's something special about this place. It feels... ancient, like it has stories of its own to tell."

As the evening wore on, the conversation shifted. The fire crackled, casting dancing shadows on the surrounding trees. Suddenly, Mia froze, her head tilted as if listening to something in the distance.

Jake: (noticing) "Mia? What's up?"

Mia held up her hand, signaling for silence. The group fell quiet, the only sound the soft rustling of leaves in the evening breeze. Then they heard it—a faint, eerie whispering carried by the wind, indistinct but undeniably present.

Mia: (whispering) "Do you hear that?"

Roz: (wide-eyed) "What is that? It sounds like voices..."

Brian: (unease creeping in) "But I don't see anyone around. Is it the wind?"

Feeling a mixture of curiosity and trepidation, Jake stood up, his eyes scanning the dense forest around them.

Jake: "Let's check it out. But stay close and be careful."

The four friends cautiously ventured into the woods, following the ethereal whispering. As they moved deeper, the sounds grew clearer, almost like a chant carried by unseen beings. The wind seemed to guide them, bending the trees in the direction they needed to go.

After a short hike, they reached a secluded clearing

by the river. The moonlight reflected off the water, creating an otherworldly glow. At the edge of the water, they saw it—a massive, cat-like creature with reptilian features, adorned with scales glistening in the moonlight. Mishipeshu, the Underwater Panther, stared at them with glowing eyes, its presence commanding and awe-inspiring.

Mia: (softly) "That's... that must be Mishipeshu. The whispers, the feeling... it all makes sense now."

Roz: (nervously) "What should we do? Approach it?"

Brian: (cautious) "I think we should show respect. This isn't a creature to challenge."

The group stood still, hearts pounding, as they watched Mishipeshu, a legendary water serpent from Ojibwe mythology. The creature's whispers faded, sounding like they were directly addressing them, completely captivating their senses. With each graceful movement, Mishipeshu commanded attention and respect. Slowly, it turned and glided back into the water, disappearing into the depths with an air of mystery and power. The clearing fell silent, leaving the friends in awe of what they had just witnessed, their minds filled with questions and a newfound reverence for the natural world and its enigmatic inhabitants.

Jake: (quietly) "We've just experienced something truly rare and powerful. Mishipeshu showed itself to us. My father once told me about the legend of this creature, but I never believed it. He said that it always whispers warnings through the trees. And now we've heard it."

Mia: (reflectively) "It's a reminder of how much we still have to learn, and how important it is to respect the mysteries of nature."

The group made their way back to camp, the whispers of the Mishipeshu still lingering in their minds. They gathered by the fire once more, their bond strengthened by the shared experience. As the night wore on, they reflected on the journey ahead, knowing that the trail held many more secrets and adventures waiting to be discovered. Mia silently wondered if this experience was an omen.

6

Shelter Critters

After crawling into their freshly dried sleeping bags and having a heartfelt prayer together, the exhausted team nestled closely on the cool wooden floor of the Gooch Gap Shelter. In the rustic shelter among the towering trees, the exhausted team found a welcome refuge from the day's harsh events. Floorboards had been worn with time, had narrow cracks between them that allowed for efficient drainage during heavy downpours, ensuring that the shelter remained dry and comfortable even during the most torrential rainstorms. The faint scent of pine permeated the air, creating a soothing atmosphere that lulled the weary hikers into a peaceful slumber.

The Appalachian Trail Council, a dedicated organization committed to maintaining shelters on the Appalachian Trail, works feverishly to ensure the safety and comfort of hikers along the trail. These shelters, strategically at various points along the trail, serve as a refuge from the unpredictable and often harsh elements that hikers may encounter during their journey. Keep in mind that these shelters, while offering weary travelers a welcome respite, are not substitutes for a home away from home. Rather, they should offer amenities such as sleeping platforms, a roof, and a privy. The Appalachian Trail Council encourages hikers to use the shelters responsibly, respecting limited space and considering fellow hikers' needs. By understanding and adhering to the purpose of these shelters, hikers can fully appreciate the valuable role they play in enhancing the Appalachian Trail experience.

There is usually a sign-in book at each shelter in which hikers can record their time there and any information they wish to leave. This sign-in book serves as a log for hikers to document their presence at the shelter, ensuring that others are aware of their whereabouts. Hikers typically include their names, dates of stay, and occasionally additional details such as the purpose of their hike or any notable experiences they encountered along the way. The sign-in book not only provides a sense of community among hikers but also serves as a valuable resource for hikers who may look for companionship or seek advice from those who have previously stayed at the shelter. The sign-in book allows authorities or search and rescue teams to gather information about hikers as a safety measure during emergencies or if someone goes missing. Overall, the sign-in book is an essential component of the shelter system, facilitating communication, safety, and camaraderie among hikers.

Each night, shelters accommodate 8–10 people. People hang backpacks from tree limbs near the shelter, freeing up space for sleeping bags on the platform. Most campers learn to share the space with others while hiking the trail.

Jake, a seasoned outdoorsman, carefully selected and cut a bundle of fresh wood for the campfire before darkness fell. With precision and expertise, he artfully arranged the logs on the already crackling flames. Positioned at the foot of the shelter, a safe distance away, the campfire provided warmth and comfort to the weary adventurers. Jake's keen eye and knowledge of fire safety prompted him to ensure that the fire remained contained within the designated area. By strategically placing additional wood on the flames, he effectively minimized the risk of the fire spreading beyond its intended boundaries. With this precautionary measure in place, the campers could relax and enjoy the mesmerizing dance of the flames, knowing that their safety was Jake's top priority.

A few hours later, Mia awakened the group with a loud screech.

Mia: "Guys, there is something large crawling all over

my face!"

Jake illuminated his lantern and announced, "Mia, I've found him."

Mia: "Great! Now how am I to go back to sleep with these things all around us?"

Roz: "Get a life, Mia. It will not hurt you. I've known about these critters for a long time, and they're harmless."

Mia: "That's real comforting, Roz."

Brian: (with frustration) "Please, everyone, can we just get back to sleep?"

Everyone quieted down, and each fell asleep at their own pace, Mia being the last.

Roz awakened the crew early (around 6 a.m.) with a crazy scream!

Roz exclaimed, "There's something in my sleeping bag! Somebody help me, please!"

Jake helped her out of her sleeping bag, and as he did, a small pack rat ran out of it.

Jake: "Nightly, they enter the shelters in search of food and warmth." Backpackers, without realizing it, drop small crumbs of food on the floorboards, and they come in to eat them. He was searching for a warm place to sleep. That's exactly why I always tell people to pack their trash in and pack it out.

The shelter critters on the Appalachian Trail include

a variety of animals that seek refuge in the natural surroundings of the trail, as well as the shelters for humans. Some of these could also share a shelter with you. These critters can range from tiny insects such as ants, beetles, and spiders to larger mammals like squirrels, raccoons, and even the occasional black bear. Birds also find shelter along the trail, with species like woodpeckers, owls, and songbirds making their nests in the trees that line the trail. Reptiles and amphibians, including snakes, turtles, and frogs, frequently find shelter in the cool, damp areas near streams and ponds. The diversity of critters that find shelter along the Appalachian Trail is a testament to the rich and thriving ecosystem that exists within this natural wilderness.

7

Black Mountain Ascent and the Fall

Daybreak came, and the group busied themselves rolling up sleeping bags, packing their equipment back in their packs, and enjoyed a quiet breakfast gathered around the campfire.

With the lost day at Gooch Gap, the team had to make suitable time today to stay on schedule with their pickup.

At 6:30 a.m., the team hit the trail beyond the open clearing at Gooch Gap, beginning their ascent up Black Mountain. The trek would be steep and exceedingly difficult, but they were determined to push forward.

Jake, the experienced team leader, expressed his estimation that covering eleven miles during the day puts the group in a splendid position to reach their destination on time. Acknowledging the importance of teamwork, Jake motivates the team to begin their journey. However, he warns that the path to the summit will not be easy, as it is steep and requires careful navigation over rocks and boulders. The recent rainfall has left the trail soaked and muddy, emphasizing the need for caution.

The team's aim is to make it to the summit within a couple of hours. Jake's estimation of their progress shows that they are on track to achieve this goal. However, the challenging terrain demands a collective effort from everyone involved.

One should not underestimate the steepness of the path. As the team ascends, it becomes crucial to observe every step, especially considering rocks and boulders. These obstacles pose potential risks, making it essential for each team member to maintain focus and remain attentive throughout the hike.

Adding to the difficulty, the recent rain has significantly affected the trail conditions. The downpour has left the path drenched, creating a layer of mud that can make it treacherous. It is imperative that the team exercises caution to prevent any accidents or injuries. This might involve slowing down the pace and taking extra care while traversing the muddy sections.

Jake's insightful estimation of their progress provides the team with a sense of optimism and motivation as they embark on their journey. By emphasizing the importance of teamwork and alertness, he ensures each member is well-prepared to overcome the challenges that lie ahead. With their collective efforts, the team is confident in reaching the summit within the expected time, despite the steepness of the trail and the muddy conditions caused by the rain.

The climb up Black Mountain was an arduous journey, testing the limits of their endurance and resolve. As they ascended, the group felt a growing sense of anticipation, each step bringing them closer to the summit. The trail was steep and unforgiving, lined with jagged rocks and narrow passages that forced them to move with caution.

The wind howled around them, and the sun cast long shadows on the rocky terrain. Jake led the way, his eyes scanning for potential hazards, while Mia and Roz followed closely behind, offering words of encouragement. Brian, usually the most adventurous of the group, was unusually quiet, his mind preoccupied with thoughts of the trail ahead.

The higher they climbed, the more treacherous the path became. Loose rocks shifted underfoot, and the sheer drops on either side made every step a calculated risk. Despite the challenges, they pressed on, driven by the promise of the breathtaking view that awaited them at the top.

As they neared the summit, the landscape changed. The

dense forests gave way to open expanses of rock, and the air grew thinner and colder. The group paused for a moment, catching their breath, and taking in the rugged beauty of their surroundings.

Jake: (panting) "We're there. Just a little further."

Mia: (smiled.) "This view better be worth it!"

Brian: (nodding) "It will be. We've come too far to turn back now."

With renewed determination, they continued their ascent. The last stretch was the most challenging, with steep inclines and unstable footing. As they navigated a narrow section, Brian felt a sudden shift in the ground beneath him.

Brian: (voice trembling) "Watch out! The rocks are loose here."

Before he could react, the ground gave way, and he slipped. In a blur of motion, he tumbled down the rocky slope, desperately trying to find something to hold on to. His friends shouted in alarm, but Brian could barely hear them over the rush of adrenaline and the roar of the wind.

Lucky for him, a sturdy tree branch jutted out from the cliff just in time, slowing his fall and bringing him to a jarring halt on a narrow ledge a few meters down. A throbbing pain in his leg caused him to despair. His mind raced with fear and determination.

Jake: (panicked) "Brian! Hold on! We're coming!"

Mia: (shouted down) "Don't move! Just stay still. We'll get to you."

As Brian lay on the ledge, he looked up at the sky; the clouds parting to reveal the midmorning light. He took a deep breath, calming his racing heart. The climb had taken an unexpected turn, and now, more than ever, he needed his friends to pull him through.

The morning light cast a soft glow on the rugged cliffs of Black Mountain. Brian's leg burned with searing pain, each throb a reminder of his precarious situation. His fingers clung to the rocky ledge, knuckles white with the effort. Above him, the voices of his friends echoed down the cliff, a lifeline of support in the unforgiving wilderness.

Brian: (gritting his teeth) "I'm not going anywhere... Just get me out of here."

Jake has already climbed down to the ledge to help Brian. The girls are trying to figure out how to get them both up safely, when a group of experienced thru hikers arrives.

Roz: "Stay calm, Jake! We'll figure something out. Just don't let go."

Jake: "Brian's losing strength, Roz! We need to hurry!"

Mia: (spotting the thru hikers) "Hey! Over here! We need your help!"

Thru-Hiker 1 (Tom): "What's going on?"

Roz: "Our friend Jake is down there with Brian. They're on a ledge about 50 feet below and we don't have enough gear to pull them up safely."

Thru-Hiker 2 (Sarah): "Don't worry, we've got this." (pulling out ropes and carabiners from her pack) "Tom, let's set up an anchored belay system."

Tom: "On it. We'll need to secure the ropes to these sturdy trees."

Roz: "Okay, I see. What do you need us to do?"

Sarah: "We'll tie a safety harness around each of them, one. You and your friend can help pull them up once we have the set. Do you have an extra rope? We sure could use one."

Roz: "Yes, I have one in my backpack. I'll get it for you."

Tom: (calling down to Jake) "Hey, Jake! I'm sending a rope down. Secure it around Brian first and we'll get you last. We'll pull both of you up safely."

Jake: "Got it. Brian, hold on tight. Help is on the way."

Brian: "I'm trying... Just a little longer, please."

Sarah: "Grab the other end of the rope ladies and help us pull when I give the signal. It's going to take all the strength we have to pull someone up from fifty feet down!"

Mia and Roz: (grabbing the rope): "Ready!"

Sarah: "Alright, 1, 2, 3... Pull!"

(Lots of grunting, pulling, and effort shown by all involved.)

Jake: "You're there, Brian. Just a few more pulls."

Brian: "I can see the top. I'm ready."

Tom: "One last heave-ho! 1, 2, 3... PULL!"

Jake and Brian: (finally reaching the top, panting heavily) "Thank you... We owe you our lives."

Sarah: "Glad we could help. Stick together out here, all right?"

Mia: "Absolutely. Thank you so much!"

Sarah: (With a cheerful smile a mile wide) "Hey, and God bless you all. This is a dangerous place, and you must always be extremely focused. Respect the trail and it will respect you."

Roz: "God bless you as well. You have saved our guys, and we'll never forget you for what you have done. We would never have done it without you guys."

Once the team reunited, Roz got busy with her first aid kit. She addressed Brian's skinned leg, applying Neosporin and bandages. Then she looked at his back and saw only one abrasion and addressed that issue. Brian also had a slight cut on his forehead, but did not need stitches, thank God.

Roz then turned her focus to the cuts and abrasions Jake had on his hands. "So, you tried being the hero again, huh, Jake? That decision you made to go down after Brian was both stupid and brave. I'm thankful that you came through the ordeal with no more injuries than you sustained. The good Lord was with you, for sure."

Once Brian and Jake's injuries were taken care of, the team made camp there for the night, not concerning themselves with reaching the next shelter a couple of miles away. They would build their fire and make a pot of army ration stew for dinner for the entire team, thankful that both Brian and Jake would be O.K.

What had just happened was a pure miracle. Jake thought of the many ways it could have gone wrong but was thankful that God had given them the strength to make it. Jake's faith was tremendous. He had been facing an impossible situation, where everything was stacked against him. Yet, against all odds, he had triumphed. It was as if a divine force had intervened, guiding his every step, and ensuring his success. Jake couldn't help but feel overwhelmed with gratitude for this incredible turn of events. The experience had only further solidified his unwavering belief in the power of faith and the existence of a higher power. Though tested, his faith remained unshakable. Jake knew he would forever carry this miraculous event in his heart, a constant reminder of the incredible things that can happen when one trusts in something greater than themselves.

As Brian and Jake embraced on the summit of Black Mountain, a wave of relief washed over Brian. He knew in that moment, without a doubt, that God had rescued him from the treacherous climb. Brian's ascent had pushed him to his physical and mental limits; this showed the power of grace. The rugged terrain and unpredictable weather had presented many challenges, testing their strength and resilience. Yet, against all odds, they had persevered. Brian couldn't help but feel a deep sense of gratitude for the immense strength and determination they had found within themselves. The summit of Black Mountain, with its breathtaking panoramic views, stood as a symbol of their triumph over adversity. As they stood there, arms wrapped tightly around each other, Brian knew that this experience had not only brought him closer to nature but also deepened his connection to a higher power. It was a humbling reminder that faced with life's greatest challenges, the grace of God can guide and protect us, empowering us to conquer any dilemma that comes our way.

Jake remembered the time that his family had been in a car wreck. It was a terrifying experience that left everyone shaken. The accident occurred on a rainy evening while they were driving home from a family gathering. As the car skidded on the wet road, it lost control and collided with a tree. Miraculously, everyone escaped from the car, except for Jake's little sister, Helen. Twisted metal held her trapped in the backseat; it confined her compact frame. Panic ensued as Jake and his family desperately tried to free her from the wreckage. In their frantic state, they called the fire rescue team for help. Time seemed to stand still as they anxiously awaited their arrival, their hearts pounding with fear for Helen's safety. Finally, the sound of sirens pierced through the chaos, signaling the rescue team. With their specialized equipment and expertise, they skillfully extricated Helen from the wreckage, ensuring her safety. The relief that washed over Jake and his family when they saw Helen being safely carried away was immeasurable. It was a reminder of the incredible bravery and dedication of the fire rescue team, who selflessly put their lives at risk to save others. The incident left a lasting impact on Jake, serving as a constant reminder of the fragility of life and the importance of cherishing the safety and well-being of loved ones.

When life is hanging in the balance, often by a thin thread, every passing second feels like an eternity. In those critical moments, we perceive mere seconds as hours because time seems to stretch endlessly. The weight of the situation amplifies the intensity of each passing moment, as if the universe itself is holding its breath, awaiting the outcome. Every decision, every action becomes crucial, as the smallest delay or hesitation can tip the scales towards either survival or tragedy. In these precarious circumstances, the concept of time becomes distorted as the mind races and the heart pounds, creating a surreal experience where each second carries the weight of an hour.

The climb up Black Mountain had become a life-threatening challenge, but it was also a testament to their resilience and camaraderie. Together, they faced the daunting task of rescuing their friend, knowing that every step counted. The trail had tested them, but it also forged their unbreakable spirit, leaving them stronger and more united for the journey ahead.

Roz and Jake embraced around the campfire and expressed their love for each other.

Roz: "Jake, I was so afraid when you descended that cliff on treacherous ground. I was mad about you doing it, but I know that your spirit is strong, and you would have it no other way. I love you so much and am just thankful to have you safe."

Jake: (compassionately) "Roz, I'm sorry that I upset you, but my bond with Brian is so strong that I would go to the ends of the earth to help him. He needed me at the most trying time of his life, and I had to respond."

Roz: (with a gleam in her eye) "You'll always be my hero, Jake. I love you."

Jake: "And I you. God made us for each other and whatever we experience on the rest of our journey over the next week and a half, we will make those together."

Mia: "Brian, do you think you can make it from here or do we need to find somebody and take you to a hospital somewhere?"

Brian: (with conviction) "I'll be O.K., Mia. I can imagine that tomorrow morning I'll be quite sore, but I'll just have to work it off. I will not allow this to stop our journey together. We've all worked extremely long and hard for this moment."

Jake: "You know, Buddy, that we will do whatever it takes for your safety. If you think for one moment that you don't want to go forward, we'll end the trip and find you a hospital."

The team sat around the campfire, basking in its glow. The temperature had dropped a good bit, and they were also on the summit of Black Mountain where the temperatures are lower than in the valleys below.

It was an uneventful night on the mountain. At first light, Jake was up and starting a fire. The team soon awakened and joined him fireside. The conversations swirled around Brian's fall, the trail experiences they had encountered, and especially the whispering trees and Mishipeshu.

8

Gooch's Grocery Store

After breaking camp, having enjoyed a breakfast of K-rations, the team packed their bags and headed down the trail. Jake, an experienced hiker and navigator, had carefully studied their route beforehand and marked it on his map. He had noticed that a highway crossing was about two miles ahead, which provided a glimmer of hope. They could find a store or a small town nearby where they could purchase more rations and seek medical help for Brian's wounds. The team felt relieved knowing that help might be within reach, and they quickened their pace, eager to reach the highway crossing.

They moved slowly because of Brian. Each step gave him excruciating pain that radiated throughout his body, leaving him grimacing with every movement. The once agile Brian now struggled to keep up with the pace, his every motion hindered by the relentless agony that consumed him. Walking, once a simple and effortless task, had become a test of endurance for Brian. His legs felt heavy and weak, as if burdened by an invisible weight. The pain he experienced was unlike anything he had ever felt before, a constant reminder of the physical limitations that now dictated his every action. Despite the overwhelming discomfort, Brian summoned all his strength to continue forward, determined not to let his condition define him. Each painstaking step he took was a testament to his resilience and unwavering determination to overcome the obstacles that stood in his way.

As they made their way through the rugged terrain, Brian needed frequent breaks to rest and catch his breath. Concerned about the well-being of her teammates, Roz took on the responsibility of monitoring their wounds. On the trail, she carefully examined both Brian and Jake's injuries to ensure they were not becoming infected. With a limited supply of bandaging left, she had to be judicious in its use, knowing that she had to make it last until they reached their destination. Despite the challenges they faced, the team's determination and Roz's vigilance kept them on track towards their goal.

Finally, the team could hear the familiar sounds of traffic ahead, signaling their nearness to Georgia Highway 60. The anticipation grew as they could sense their destination drawing closer. Jake, with his keen eyesight, spotted the highway first and couldn't contain his excitement. With a sense of relief and gratitude, he exclaimed, "Praise the Lord! I see the highway. We've made it!" The team's perseverance and determination had paid off, as they had successfully navigated through unfamiliar territory to reach their desired destination.

At the highway crossing, Mia noticed public restrooms on the opposite side, male and female. The facilities were much nicer than the rustic outhouses along the trail.

A gray, 1979 Ford Van pulled off the road near the restrooms, and a middle-aged man and woman got out of the front, along with a son and daughter, from the backseat. The kids were in their teens.

The father called out to Jake. "Hey, son, where are you going today?"

Jake immediately went over to the man and began talking, so typical of Jake.

Jake: "We have been on the walk of a lifetime and have lived to tell it, Sir. A couple of miles back up on Black Mountain, my friend Brian here fell fifty feet onto a rocky ledge and sustained quite a few scrapes and bumps. Luckily, we could save him with the help of some other thru hikers who came to our aid."

Man: "Wow! Sounds like a harrowing experience! I'm Bob Warren and this is my wife, Marlene, and our two children, Heather, and Bill. We just left Dahlonega and are heading to Blue Ridge for a week of vacation. We're from Athens, Georgia."

Marlene: "Son, are you sure that you're O.K.? You appear to be frazzled. I can see the weariness in your eyes."

Jake: "Ma'am, we're O.K., but we sure could use a respite for a while."

Bob: "Then that does it. At the foot of the mountain sits an old country store called "Gooch's Grocery." If you'll just wait for us to use the facilities here, we'll be good to go."

Roz: "Thank you so much, Sir. That would certainly be wonderful. We need supplies like food, fresh water for our canteens, and some medical supplies for wound treatment. You guys are a godsend."

Mia: "Are you sure that we can get all of our equipment and us into your van?"

Bob: "No problem, dear. There's plenty of room for you."

With that, everyone used the facilities at the rest stop, loaded up the van with their camping gear and supplies, and eagerly embarked on their journey down the mountainside towards the charming town of Suches, Georgia. The van skillfully maneuvered down the winding road, providing the team with breathtaking views of the surrounding lush forests and rolling hills. After a thrilling descent, the van finally came to a stop in front of Gooch's Grocery, a beloved local establishment. The friendly family who owned the van wished the team god-speed, and bid them farewell, leaving them standing in awe in front of the rustic clapboarded building.

The store exuded a charming and nostalgic atmosphere, with its weathered exterior and a section to the side dedicated to a plentiful supply of neatly cut and stacked cords of wood. This section served as a testament to the store's commitment to serving both the local community and the adventurous backpackers who frequented the area. Excitement filled the air as the team eagerly prepared to explore this quaint little store and all the adventures that awaited them in the beautiful wilderness of Suches, Georgia.

Across the road, in front of the store, the team could see a large, beautiful lake. It stretched out glistening under the warm sunlight. The lake was a mesmerizing sight, with its clear water inviting anyone who laid eyes on it to take a dip. It was mirror-like, perfectly reflecting the small hills that surrounded it. Hills, covered in lush greenery, added to the picturesque scene, creating a breathtaking panorama. The occasional ripple caused by a gentle breeze only interrupted the tranquility of the lake, making it a serene oasis amidst the small township. The team stood there in awe, captivated by the natural beauty before them.

"You kids come on inside!" the owner's wife yelled from the front entrance. "We got everything you need."

She introduced herself at the door. "I'm Imagene Gooch, married to this old man Pete, here. He's a rascal if ever there was one. Take nothing he tells you as the gospel truth. You kids doing the trail?"

Jake: "Yes, ma'am, we are. Started at Amicalola Falls and headed to Fontana Dam. Just a two-week trip during our spring break from Young Harris."

Imagene: "You know, that's a wonderful school. Had a cousin who went there many moons ago. She did something like you are doing with three other classmates. Time of her life, she used to say every time we'd talk about it. That girl ain't quite right, you know. Been in and out of hospitals for years."

Mia: "What's wrong with her, ma'am?"

Imagene: "Oh, some say she heard voices on the trail and even slept with the devil himself one night!"

Pete: "You're telling me you're getting off at Fontana, kids?"

Roz: "Yes sir. We hope to make it that far. Seems like everything is working against us, but we're determined to make it as far as we can with the time we're allotted. We almost lost Brian yesterday up on Black Mountain."

Pete: "What happened?"

Jake recalled the entire event from the previous day while all four walked around inside Gooch's Grocery. Brian kept eyeing the critters hanging up on the walls. There was a "Jack-a-Lope," a Jack Rabbit with wings, a Flying Possum, a stuffed turkey, and a couple of large Buck Deer heads with many points on each. Jake took a second look at the Jack-a-Lope and asked Pete about it.

Pete: "Yea, that's my little Jack-a-Lope. They are rare round here, but I know they are plenty out in Texas."!!

Imagene: "You old fool. Leave them kids be. You keep telling everybody bout that stuffed animal, and you know they come from Australia and not Texas."

Pete: "That's my little Jack-a-Lope I shot up on Hightower Ridge one night while hunting with some friends. We were up there trying to trap snipes when he crossed the little road in front of us. I took my old shotgun and brought him down."

The team had a good laugh over that one! Brian knew it wasn't real but wasn't sure if Pete did!

Imagene: "We get kids like you about every day. Some will come down this dirt road by the store that comes down the hill from Gooch Gap. Seems like it storms up there every night or so and they make their way here. Why, we've put no telling how many up for the night during the storms in our little garage out back. Good kids but scared of our kinds of thunderstorms."

Roz: "Do any of them ever mention hearing strange voices up there?"

Pete: "Ah, sure! I've heard them voices all my life. Some people think that it's the voices of Civil War soldiers who died in these hollows and on these ridges. Ain't gonna hurt you. They are just the saints of the past whose spirits still linger."

Imagene: "I done told you, fool, not to tell these kids about that crazy old legend. Ain't no spirits up there, less you take it up there with you."

The kids stocked up their supplies and Jake even bought a new pair of hiking boots. He had busted part of the sole off one shoe and thought this to be the best opportunity to replace them. The store counter had quite a few breakfast sandwiches, so the crew bought one each. There were sausage biscuits, ham, and egg biscuits, or just bacon and egg biscuits. Three of them enjoyed a nice cold soft drink, but Roz, the health-conscious one, had a bottle of cranberry juice.

After they had stocked up, Pete asked if he could take them back up the mountain to the gap they had come from. Sure, was the excited answer from the team.

As they left the store in the back of Pete's old pickup, Pete had a question for Mia and Roz.

Pete: "Did you girls see him? Did you see my panther? Mishipeshu?"

Roz: (with surprise) "We did. We kept hearing this voice on the wind and then followed the voice to the river and watched him come in and out of the river. It was a weird-looking creature, Pete. Do you see him often?"

Pete: "Yes, ma'am, he is weird, and only so many have ever seen him. My daddy said that he was an omen, a creature that alarmed hikers and hunters of an upcoming death or something."

Pete continued. "Did something happen to you after you heard and seen him?"

Mia: "Yes it did, Sir. Our friend Brian slipped and fell over the cliff on top of Black Mountain, and we had to rescue him. Thank goodness some other thru hikers came along and helped, but it was touch-and-go there for a long while."

Pete: "Ya'll need to be incredibly careful when you hit the trail again. That fall may be just the beginning of danger lurking ahead."

As Pete pulled to the side of the road at the crossing, the team jumped out and waved goodbye, and continued the trail after a brief restroom stop at the latrines.

Very rough hiking lay ahead for the team as they made their way towards the Blood Mountain shelter. With several miles to go and with Brian's leg, it would take longer than usual, so they pushed ahead with fervor to reach their destination. They had about four miles to make it to Woods Hole Shelter for the night. It was already 2 p.m., so they would need to hustle, since sundown came around 5:30 p.m. in the mountains.

Arriving at Woods Hole Shelter, a popular resting spot along the Appalachian Trail, the team was disappointed to find it already filled with hikers seeking refuge. With no room available, they had to produce an alternative sleeping arrangement. Fortunately, Jake had the foresight to purchase a tarp at Gooch's Store in Suches prior to their journey. Using his resourcefulness, Jake ingeniously devised a lean-to structure using the tarp, providing the team with a sheltered spot to sleep under. Previous campers thankfully cleared a suitable area, and many sturdy trees enabled secure tarp tie-offs. As the night air grew colder, Brian suggested the idea of building a fire to keep warm.

Eager to help, Jake readily agreed to take on the task. With his trusty saw, he skillfully cut a few branches he found nearby, while the girls diligently gathered broken limbs and pitch to serve as kindling. Once all the elements were in place, Jake reached into his backpack and pulled out one of his reliable firebugs, a handy tool that never failed to ignite a flame. With a flick of his wrist, the fire roared to life, casting a warm glow, and providing much-needed comfort to the weary hikers.

After a long and challenging day of hiking, the team settled down at their campsite to enjoy a well-deserved meal. They had cooked a delicious and satisfying meal using K-rations, which provided them with the nutrition and energy to fuel their bodies. As they sat around the crackling campfire, their faces illuminated by the warm glow, they recounted the events of the day. They reminisced about their journey from the summit of Black Mountain, where they had witnessed breathtaking panoramic views, to their visit to Gooch's Grocery in the quaint town of Suches. At Gooch's Grocery, they had restocked their supplies and indulged in some local treats, rejuvenating their spirits for the rest of their adventure. After leaving the grocery store, they embarked on a thrilling ride back up the mountain, their hearts pounding with excitement as they navigated the winding roads. Finally, they arrived back at their campsite, ready to continue their hike and conquer the next leg of their journey.

Roz: "Oh, by the way, you guys didn't hear Pete asking us about Mishipeshu. He told us it was a panther, and it usually warned campers of some foreboding event."

Jake: "Did you guys really believe anything that old man said?"

Mia: "I believed him, Jake. Do you think any of our friends back at Young Harris would ever believe such a crazy story? I can hear them now, laughing and dismissing it as nonsense. They would say things like, 'They're crazy,' or 'Ah, they haven't seen such a creature!' Our trip would become the talk of the town, with everyone labeling it as a wild adventure. The incredulous looks on their faces, as we recount our encounter with the mysterious creature, would be priceless. Our friends would surely think we had lost our minds, unable to comprehend the extraordinary experiences we had. But deep down, I know what we saw was real, and no amount of skepticism from others can change that."

Jake: "You're right, Mia. A story like that should remain with us and not told to everyone else. It was real, for all four of us saw the creature."

Roz: "I agree, Jake. We know what we saw, but others would never believe it in a million years. Do you guys not realize that we witnessed something grand and mystical? I'll never forget it as long as I live."

As the night wore on and the flames flickered, the team of adventurous hikers stopped for the day, having already rolled out their cozy sleeping bags. Exhaustion overcame them, yet their hearts thrilled with accomplishment and anticipation of what awaited. The day's journey included breathtaking landscapes, challenging terrains, and unexpected wildlife encounters. Each step along the trail had brought them closer to nature and closer to each other.

As they drifted off to sleep, their minds filled with vivid dreams, they couldn't help but reflect on the unforgettable experiences they had shared. Their team bond, the awe-inspiring sights, and the physical and mental challenges they overcame would forever remain in their memories. This expedition thus far had not only tested their endurance and determination, but it had also opened their eyes to the beauty and resilience of the natural world. They knew that what they had experienced so far on the trail would be with them for life, shaping their perspectives and inspiring them to seek more adventures in the great outdoors.

9

New Day, Old Trail

Mia was the first one to stir. She crawled out of her sleeping bag and made her way to the potty behind the shelter. The early morning was covered with dense fog and mist, typical for the Appalachian Trail. She wondered about Brian and his leg and would check on him when she returned from the potty.

As Mia left the potty, she encountered a young man named Wilson who was just standing in the trail looking around and stretching. He bent over and back up again and again and Mia assumed that he was exercising. Without being rude, Mia says Good morning to the guy.

Wilson: "Good morning to you as well. Not a particularly beautiful morning, wouldn't you say?"

Mia: "No, not really. It's a bit foggy and dreary looking."

Wilson: "Oh, it'll clear out in an hour or so. This happens almost every day here on the trail. I'm just doing my routine work-out before the crowd gets up. We've been on the trail now for three days. Started out at Unicoi Gap and are headed for Amicalola. James and Darryl are my three friends from Georgia Tech in Atlanta, and we do these hikes together once each year. We're all in the engineering school there."

Mia: "That's great, Wilson. I'm with the team over there at that makeshift lean-to. We're all students at Young Harris College in Young Harris, Georgia. We've been on the trail for five days now and headed from Amicalola to Fontana Dam."

Wilson: "That's great, Mia. I had a friend once who attended Young Harris and then transferred to Georgia Tech to finish his degree program. It's a great little school."

Mia: "Have you see anything spectacular on the trail?"

Wilson: "We sure have. Last night at Blood Mountain, we witnessed one of the most spectacular sights I've ever seen. The entire sky lit up with millions of lightning bugs! I hear that they do that during the early spring during mating season. It was literally fantastic!"

Wilson continued eagerly to share. "My friend James almost stepped on a Copperhead Mocassin crossing the trail, and Darryl saw a black bear late yesterday evening while filling his canteen with water at the creek below here. Have you guys had anything happen along the trail?"

Mia: "Our friend Brian slipped on the edge of Black Mountain a couple of days ago and fell about 50 feet below and landed on a ledge. We had to rescue him with ropes and harnesses provided by some thru hikers. He skinned up one of his legs badly and received quite a few scrapes and bruises."

Mia contained herself and tried hard not to mention the voices or the sighting of Mishipeshu.

Wilson: "I'm thankful that your friend is O.K. How's his walking?"

Mia: "It's slow, but he's gonna make it, we hope."

Wilson: "Well, nice talking with you, Mia. I see that my crew is up and getting ready to hike so I better go. Listen, have a safe journey. My prayers will be with you."

Mia: "Thanks, Wilson, and the same with you, James, and Darryl. Hope we meet again some day."

With that, Mia returned to a busy crew taking down the tarp and getting their packs ready to go.

Brian: "Who were you talking to out there, Mia?"

Mia: "Just some guy I met on the trail who was up and exercising. He's with two other friends who stayed in the shelter last night. They are students at Georgia Tech. Nice fellow. He shared a few stories of the trail with me."

Jake: "You didn't tell him about the creature we saw, did you?"

Mia: "Of course not, Jake! I bit my tongue though because I wanted to tell someone about it so badly. That's just one of those life-altering events that is hard to keep to yourself."

Jake: "O.K., team. Our goal today is to hike down to the Walasi-Yi Center at the base of Blood, Mountain. I understand it to be a great little camping gear and supply store, so we'll take a break there before we make the great ascent up Blood Mountain. It's going to be a long day, what with Brian's leg and all, but we'll make it. I have complete confidence in our team."

Mia checked in with Brian and Roz came over to look at his leg wound.

Mia: "How's it feeling, Brian?"

Brian: "It's very sore, Mia, but I can make it, I think. Best give it a try at least."

Mia gave Brian a big hug and kiss and then prepared her backpack for the day's journey. The trail ahead of them was rough with plenty of ups and downs, switch-backs and turns. The team allowed Brian to lead the way at his own pace, making sure that he did not overdo it. They would stop whenever he felt the need, then venture forward at his command. The team had worked together beautifully and had more adventures awaiting them up that rocky trail.

Jake noticed a stream sign along the trail and knew they

had to have water, so he and Roz took off down the tiny trail to the stream below. Mia and Brian thought it was a good opportunity for Jake and Roz to have some alone time.

The stream was very small and filled with plenty of water and salamanders. Jake also saw a hellbender in the water, partially hidden beneath a rock. He tried to catch it, but it eluded him.

Roz: "You better leave that thing alone, Jake. It could hurt you."

Jake: "Ah, Babe, I've caught these little critters before. They are harmless and fun to play with and look at."

About that time Jake caught one of the black salamanders and held it up for Roz to look at.

Roz: "Jake Sutton, you're a fool! Didn't I tell you not to pick those things up? What if they have some kind of disease?"

Jake: "Look at this beautiful creature, Roz. He's one of God's special critters."

With that, the two gathered and filtered enough water to fill the four canteens and began making their trek back up the mountainside, being careful to look on either side for any slithering creatures that might be about. Midway up the mountain, Roz heard the voices again. The wind was whispering and very blusterous. She became suddenly aware that they were not alone. Jake heard the voices as well. The two stood there in an embrace on the trail, and a waited for whatever might happen next. The voices were shrill and would come and go across the wind, creating an eerie presence that Jake and Roz could not see but only hear.

And just like that, the voices stopped. As Jake and Roz headed up the trail, the voices would return, but they continued their trek to meet up with Brian and Mia at the trailhead. They shared the experience with Brian and Mia when they returned and wondered what it could mean.

All day those voices would follow them, reminding them they were not alone in the vastness of the mountains. They provoked a strange feeling with each team member, a mix of curiosity and unease. As the team took a much-needed break near a picturesque clearing, they eagerly shed their heavy backpacks and found spots to rest. Jake, the team's resident adventurer, always seeking unique experiences, perched himself on a massive fallen log from an ancient oak tree. Little did he know, this decision would lead to a heart-stopping encounter.

As soon as Jake settled onto the log, it shifted beneath his weight, causing a commotion that sent everyone into a panic. From under the log emerged a Copperhead Mocassin, a venomous snake, accompanied by a brood of several babies. The sight was enough to send a shiver down the spines of even the bravest members of the team. In a split second, Jake reacted, leaping away from the danger and prompting everyone to scramble up the hill, far from the slithering creatures.

But Jake, ever the Boy Scout, quickly composed himself and reached for his trusty wooden cane. With utmost care, he gingerly picked up each snake, one by one, and gently tossed them away from the log. The team watched in awe as he deftly handled the dangerous reptiles, counting ten tiny babies in total. Having safely moved the snakes, the group regrouped, their hearts still pounding, and hastily retrieved their backpacks, eager to escape the unexpected danger.

Roz, still shaken from the ordeal, couldn't help but express her concern to Jake. "Jake, one of those snakes could have easily bitten you! How crazy is that? Huh?" she exclaimed, her voice laced with worry.

Jake, unfazed by the close call, replied calmly, "No problem, Roz. I have had several encounters with snakes in my lifetime, and my father taught me how to handle them. I'm sorry if I disturbed you over it."

As the team gathered their belongings and prepared to resume their trek, two figures approaching along the trail caught their attention. The hikers, a husband-and-wife duo in their sixties, introduced themselves as John and Lenora Patrick from Warm Springs, Georgia. The team welcomed the couple warmly, grateful for fellow adventurers amidst the rugged wilderness of the mountains.

Mia, an outdoor enthusiast, excitedly shared her recent moccasin adventure with the couple. She warned them to be extra vigilant as they continued their journey, advising them to keep an eye out for any snakes that might lurk in their path. John, a member of the couple, chimed in and informed the team that they had already encountered not one, but two Copperhead snakes along their way. He explained that these venomous reptiles were emerging from their winter hibernation to bask in the warm sunshine. The couple, who were counselors at the historic Warm Springs Rehab Center, were familiar with the area's rich history. The center had gained popularity many years ago when President Roosevelt sought treatment there for his polio. With this knowledge in mind, the couple continued their journey, filled with both excitement and caution.

John said, "Gotta go, guys. Nice meeting you. We've got to keep our schedule tight. Our friends will meet us at the Highway 60 crossing and take us back to Warm Springs."

The team continued their trek up the mountain with much more caution than usual. They were now more fully aware of a new kind of danger the mountains held in store for them. They would take another break at Slaughter Gap and walk down the path to the streams below. There, Jake would again play in the water, citing more salamanders as he would overturn rocks to find them. He also pulled out a large crayfish from a section of the stream and everyone was impressed and had to examine the critter.

The trek from Woods Hole to Neel's Gap was marked on Jake's map as 3.5 miles. It was the toughest stretch of the trail so far, especially for poor Brian who struggled with each step. But Brian was made of tough material, having grown up doing hard work on his father's farm. He was his father's second man-in-charge before he had left for college. He knew he could make the trip after his fall and rescue, so he pushed himself forward.

Jake had found several large snails along the trail and had put them in a ziplock plastic bag telling the team that he was going to roast them that night around the campfire. They were in disgust as he talked about how delicious they would be. He reminded them that it was Escargot, a delicacy in most countries of the world, yet they were still not impressed, thinking only about how slimy they appeared to be.

The trek from Woods Hole to Neel's Gap was a challenging 3.5-mile journey, as indicated on Jake's map. This stretch of the trail proved to be the toughest thus far, especially for Brian, who struggled with each step. However, despite the difficulties, Brian's resilience and determination shone through. Growing up on his father's farm, he was no stranger to hard work and had even held the position of his father's second-in-command before leaving for college. With this background, Brian knew he had the strength to complete the trip, even after his recent fall and subsequent rescue.

During the hike, Jake stumbled upon several large snails along the trail. Being an adventurous and curious soul, he collected them and placed them in a secure ziplock plastic bag. To the team's dismay, Jake proudly announced that he intended to roast the snails over the campfire that night. He eagerly described how delicious escargot, a delicacy in many countries, could be. However, his companions were far from impressed. Their focus shifted from the potential culinary experience to the slimy appearance of the snails, causing a sense of disgust among the group.

Jake, a mischievous and curious individual, found immense pleasure in irritating his group with his intriguing discoveries. His insatiable desire to provoke reactions from others fueled his passion for sharing his findings, no matter how trivial or significant they may be. In fact, he took great joy in observing the various remarks and responses his revelations elicited from his companions.

Jake's enthusiasm for annoying his group with his find-ings stemmed from his innate need for attention and val-idation. Whether it was a peculiar fact he stumbled upon during his extensive research or a thought-provoking ob-servation he made during his everyday encounters, Jake would embrace any opportunity to captivate his audience. His ability to present his discoveries in a manner that both entertained and provoked his companions was truly re-markable.

One cannot deny that Jake's relentless pursuit of irritat-ing his group with his findings was also driven by a sense of pride. He relished knowing that he possessed a unique perspective and a keen eye for detail, which allowed him to uncover hidden gems others might overlook. With every remark made by his peers, Jake felt a surge of satisfaction, knowing that his findings had successfully stirred their curiosity or ignited a lively debate.

Jake's enjoyment in annoying the group with his find-ings was not purely self-serving. He believed that by shar-ing his discoveries, he was enriching the collective knowl-edge and stimulating intellectual growth within the group. Through his persistent efforts, he hoped to create an en-vironment where everyone felt compelled to explore new ideas and expand their horizons.

A combination of seeking attention, pride in his unique

perspective, and a genuine desire to foster intellectual growth fueled Jake's penchant for annoying the group with his findings. While some may view his behavior as irritating, the value he brought to the group was dynamic. Jake's ability to entertain, provoke, and inspire his companions with his intriguing discoveries made him an indispensable member of the group, ensuring that their discussions were always engaging and thought-provoking.

Jake had always been an adventurous and curious child. While his playmates would happily swing and slide on the playgrounds, Jake's restless spirit compelled him to explore the unknown. From a young age, he had a natural inclination towards discovering new things and pushing the boundaries of his comfort zone. Whether it was venturing into uncharted territories in the neighborhood or delving into the depths of his imagination, Jake was always seeking to uncover the mysteries that lay beyond the surface. His insatiable thirst for knowledge and his unwavering determination set him apart from his peers. As he grew older, this inherent curiosity would continue to shape his life and lead him on incredible journeys of discovery. Whether it was exploring remote corners of the world or delving into the complexities of scientific research, Jake's innate sense of wonder and his unwavering desire to explore the unknown would always be a defining characteristic of his personality.

Mia: "You are crazy, Jake, if you think I am going to eat one of those snails! It will never touch my lips, I can guarantee you that."

Jake: "Ah, Mia, they are really delicious and will just pop out of their shells once I put them in the ashes beside the fire."

Mia: "No way, Jose! You can gladly give them to Roz or Brian. I don't even want to touch them!"

Roz, who had more experience in wilderness survival, warned Jake that eating things found along the trail was not a good idea because of potential health hazards. She mentioned the possibility of contamination or parasites that could cause serious illnesses. Jake, however, dismissed her concerns, stating confidently, "You guys are just wussies! There's absolutely nothing wrong with the snails. My dad and I have eaten them on various occasions in the past and they were delicious." Despite Jake's reassurances, Mia remained unconvinced and stood firm in her decision to avoid the snails.

10

Blood Mountain Memories

C ontinuing their journey towards the Walasi-Yi Center, in the beautiful North Georgia mountains, the team of hikers enthusiastically sang a few popular Christian songs they had remembered from their weekly Campus Crusade for Christ meetings. Among the heartfelt melodies, "Kumbaya" resonated with them the most, filling their spirits with renewed energy and determination. Despite the challenging terrain, their harmonious voices echoed through the wilderness, serving as a constant reminder of their shared faith and the support they provided for one another. However, Brian, one of the team members, was struggling with each additional step. Despite his physical limitations, the team supported and encouraged Brian, preventing anyone from being left behind on this arduous but meaningful journey.

Brian: "You guys know that I dearly love each of you, and I appreciate all the help and encouragement you have been giving me. I'm gonna make it, and we'll stand together at trail's end."

Jake: "That a boy! That's the attitude I would expect from my best-man to be."

Brian had already agreed, without hesitation, to be the best man at Jake and Roz's wedding. It was two years off, but he would always stand by his best friend. The two had really grown close over the past four years at Young Harris, a small liberal arts college nestled in the picturesque North Georgia mountains. From the moment they met as wide-eyed freshmen, Brian and Jake had formed an unbreakable bond. They shared countless late-night study sessions, spontaneous road trips, and even a few wild adventures that made their college experience truly unforgettable.

They built their friendship on trust, loyalty, and a deep understanding of each other's dreams and aspirations. They had supported one another through thick and thin, celebrating each other's successes and offering a shoulder to lean on during tough times. Brian had always been there for Jake, cheering him on during his soccer matches, helping him through heartbreaks, and even giving him a safe space to vent about the pressures of college life.

That's why, without second thoughts, Jake had mustered his way down the treacherous mountainside to rescue Brian when he fell up on Black Mountain. Despite the imminent danger and exhaustion, their profound connection fueled Jake's unwavering determination to save his best friend. He knew that Brian would have done the same for him without hesitation.

Their bond was a testament to the power of genuine friendship, a bond that transcends time and distance. As they looked forward to Jake and Roz's wedding, the ultimate celebration of love and commitment, Brian couldn't help but feel a surge of gratitude for having such an incredible friend by his side. Being the best man was not just a title or an obligation; it was an opportunity to honor the remarkable friendship they had built and to continue supporting each other as they embarked on this new chapter in their lives.

Steep inclines, craggy rock faces, and difficult terrain laced the trek from Woody Gap to Blood Mountain in Georgia's Chattahoochee National Forest. As part of the renowned Appalachian Trail, this section of the hike offered a thrilling and challenging experience for outdoor enthusiasts. The trail meandered through dense forests, occasionally opening to breathtaking vistas of the surrounding valleys and peaks. Along the way, there were several conveniently located pull-off sites that provided hikers with the opportunity to pause, catch their breath, and admire the awe-inspiring beauty of the natural landscape. These lookout points offered panoramic views, allowing visitors to soak in the grandeur of the mountains and take in the wilderness's vastness. The combination of the arduous terrain and the stunning scenery made this trek an unforgettable adventure for those seeking a rewarding and immersive hiking experience.

The journey from Woods Hole to the summit of Blood Mountain was short, but the final mile proved to be quite challenging. Despite the difficulties, the team persevered and pushed forward. They couldn't help but feel some regrets about taking on this hike, especially during the last stretch.

Brian faced the most difficulty. His leg continued to burn, regardless of the generous amount of Neosporin that Roz had applied. Every step was a painful reminder of his injury. He summoned all his strength and determination to keep walking.

It felt like the steep incline would never end, pushing the team to their limits. The terrain was rugged, with rocks and tree roots making the ascent even more treacherous. Fatigue set in, but the team refused to give up.

The stunning natural beauty surrounding them provided some respite from the physical strain. Towering trees offered patches of shade, offering brief moments of relief from the scorching sun. The distant sound of chirping birds and the rustling leaves created a serene atmosphere, momentarily distracting them from the physical demands of the hike.

As they ascended higher, the air grew cooler and thinner. Each breath became a conscious effort, as if the mountain itself were challenging their lungs. Despite the discomfort, the team couldn't help but marvel at the breathtaking views that unfolded before them. The panoramic vista of the surrounding mountains and valleys was awe-inspiring, reminding them why they embarked on this adventure.

Finally, after what felt like an eternity, the team reached the summit of Blood Mountain. Exhausted but exhilarated, they respected the majestic scenery that stretched out before them. The sense of accomplishment and the satisfaction of conquering the challenging hike washed away any lingering doubts or regrets.

As they took a moment to catch their breath and soak in the surrounding beauty, the team realized that the hardships they faced were worth it. The journey to the summit of Blood Mountain had not only tested their physical strength, but also their determination and resilience. It was a reminder that sometimes the most rewarding experiences are born out of perseverance and pushing beyond one's comfort zone.

With a renewed sense of accomplishment and a new-found respite, the hikers noticed the white stone cottage built for thru hikers and set up their sleeping bags for the evening inside. There was ample space for twenty hikers or more inside, and the area on top of Blood Mountain was spectacular.

Jake immediately rekindled the fire left behind by other hikers and cut additional wood with Roz's help. He had learned in Boy Scouts to cut from dead growth and never from live trees. The two worked together conscientiously to secure enough wood for the night and carried it back to camp.

The team stood on the Blood Mountain overlooked, fittingly named "Picnic Rock," while Brian hugged Mia and Jake hugged Roz. Both couples looked out over the valleys and vistas before them. Giving God praise in that moment, the four renewed their love for each other.

Blood Mountain has had a rich and eerie history. It stands as the highest peak on the Georgia section of the A.T. at 4,461 feet. There are kinds of rumors about how it got its name, from a battle that took place among native tribes living in the area, to the reddish color of the lichen and Catawba rhododendron living there on top of the mountain. The Cherokee saw the place as the home of the

Immortals, a friendly race of spirit people.

After securing their sleeping quarters and taking out their food for the evening, the group of adventurers gathered around the roaring fire that Jake and Roz had skillfully built. The crackling flames provided a comforting warmth as the night air grew colder. As the group settled in, Jake reached into his bag and pulled out a container filled with the snails. With a mischievous grin, he carefully placed them by the edge of the fire, causing a few of his companions to wrinkle their noses in disgust.

Unfazed by their reactions, Jake patiently waited as the snails cooked in the coals. Eventually, the tantalizing aroma filled the air, piquing the curiosity of his comrades. With a sly smile, Jake cracked open one of the cooked snails and offered it to Roz, who promptly declined with a disgusted expression. She warned about parasites or diseases in the snails, echoing an earlier warning. The rest of the group, wary of the unconventional meal, opted to stick to their K-rations for dinner.

Undeterred by his friends' hesitation, Jake shrugged off their reservations, proclaiming that he had eaten snails before with no ill effects. With a bold declaration, he declared the snails tasted even better with a dash of spicy sauce. Despite his attempts to convince the others, they remained steadfast in their decision to pass on the peculiar delicacy.

As the night wore on, the group continued to enjoy the warmth of the fire, sharing stories and laughter. While the prospect of trying snails cooked over an open fire has intrigued some, they left Jake to his own culinary adventure.

A team of thru hikers, who were on their long-distance hiking journey, arrived at the campsite during that time. They settled their backpacks and camping gear in the cozy cottage before joining Jake and his crew. This adventurous group comprised three girls and two guys, all of whom were taking a break from their studies at Kennesaw State University, above Atlanta, near Interstate 75. One girl, Ruby, noticed snails nearby on the edge of the fire, and expressed her interest in having one. With curiosity, she delicately cracked open a snail shell and extracted the small, rubbery creature inside and began chewing on it. This peculiar act caused Mia, Brian, and Roz to feel a mixture of surprise and disgust. However, Jake, ever the accommodating host, had an abundant supply of snails and gladly shared them with Ruby's companions. The thru hikers, grateful for the chance to indulge in a lavish meal and enjoy the company of fellow campers, eagerly joined the gathering.

Just as the evening was settling in, four other middle-aged individuals arrived at the campsite. They set up their sleeping quarters in the nearby cabin, adding to the growing sense of camaraderie and adventure in this picturesque outdoor haven.

Roy was the team leader and was a rugged-looking type that fit well with a seasoned backpacker. He and Jake, who also had a strong background in scouting, shared Boy Scout adventures with each other, reminiscing about their days of camping, hiking, and honing their survival skills. Meanwhile, the other team members, Roz, Brian, and Mia, were eager to hear about the day's hike and share their own experiences. Ruby's team had set off from Amicalola three days prior and had already made it to this point on the trail. The sheer speed and determination with which they had covered the distance left Jake's team in awe. They couldn't believe that Ruby's team had walked such a long distance in such a short amount of time. As the four campers from Ruby's team joined them, everyone gathered around, excited to exchange stories and share their many adventures along the trail. They particularly recounted the thunderstorm they had encountered at Hawk Mountain, which forced them to seek refuge by hiking down the Georgia Power dirt road to Gooch's Grocery. Grateful for the store owner's kindness, they were allowed to spend most of the night in the store's garage, safe from the elements.

Jake: "Yea, we talked to the old couple running the store

yesterday, and they said that folks would come in there and spend the night to get dry. What did you think about the old couple?"

Mark: "They were really a hoot! Loved hearing their accents and stories about the Jack-a-Lope and flying possum. Did they tell you guys the same stories?"

Brian: "Yea. We endured those funny tales, knowing that he was making it all up. He seemed to relish in the tales, so we didn't argue with him. He was extremely helpful and brought us back up to Woody Gap after we bought fresh supplies."

The old couple running the store was a delightful and memorable duo. Their charming accents added a touch of authenticity to the quaint store in the remote woods. They entertained the team with their amusing stories about mythical creatures like the Jack-a-Lope and flying possum. Even though we knew they were just tall tales, their enthusiasm captivated us. They took immense pleasure in sharing these imaginative stories with anyone who would listen. Despite the fantastical nature of their tales, the old couple proved to incredibly helpful. After we purchased our much-needed supplies, they kindly offered to drive us back up to Woody Gap, ensuring we had a safe journey ahead. Their generosity and warmth made our experience at the store even more memorable.

That night in the cozy cottage, an unexpected and ca-cophonous disturbance abruptly shattered the peaceful silence. An uproar that resembled the deafening rumble of a thunderstorm shattered the tranquility of the evening. However, upon closer inspection, the source of the com-motion was not nature's fury, but the resonating snores of two unfortunate individuals. These snorers, hailing from different teams, produced a symphony of nasal vibrations that reverberated through the cottage, causing the sturdy roof to tremble as if on the verge of collapse. The deci-bel levels reached such heights that it appeared the walls themselves might burst at any moment. The unfortunate consequences of this symphony of snores were clear as the exhausted team members struggled to find solace in the arms of sleep.

Amidst the chaos, they found moments of respite, al-lowing their weary bodies to rejuvenate and recharge. As dawn broke and the first rays of sunlight filtered through the windows, Mia, Roz, Brian, and Jake reluctantly bid farewell to the other teams, who were already preparing for their departure. With heavy hearts, they gathered their belongings, shouldered their backpacks, and embarked on a northward journey. However, Jake, ever the adventurous spirit, contemplated a detour. Seeking to create some dis-tance between themselves and the other teams, he and the team lingered a while longer atop the magnificent summit, savoring the breathtaking vistas and relishing in the solitude before their descent from Blood Mountain.

Because it had turned very cold during the night, the team wore their warmest attire. In just a few minutes, it began snowing; softly at first, and then harder. Brian and the team went back inside the cottage to wait it out, not knowing how long it would last. The snowfall covered every tree in white and the ground in snow as an hour, two hours, three hours passed. Jake finally decided, because of the lateness of the morning, that the team would just remain at the cottage overnight. He felt that the snow would end before morning. He busied himself with getting the fire going again, and the team stood around it, enjoying the falling snow.

Suddenly, the sky lit up with a strange glow of lights. Mia, the horticulturist said that it was fireflies. They were everywhere, a true remarkable sight. Jake asked what it was and Mia, a student of biology and all things plant and animal, said that the phenomenon was called Bioluminescence. It was mating season for the fireflies, and they were in full array.

That night was quiet and peaceful; no snoring campers to rattle the walls. Everyone received a much-needed sleep. The snow stopped around 10 p.m.

The following morning at daybreak, Jake went out to stoke the fire for the team to warm by. Indeed, the snow had stopped and was already beginning to melt.

Mia, a passionate nature enthusiast and student of Horticulture, meticulously surveyed the rich and diverse flora and fauna that adorned the pristine summit. Meanwhile, Jake and Brian, the team's handy lumberjacks, skillfully wielded their trusty saws to cut up more wood. Their thoughtful act should leave behind a sufficient supply of firewood for the next group of adventurous campers. Roz, an organized and eco-conscious member of the team, diligently cleaned out her backpack and carefully bagged the shells from the snails that Jake had collected during their exploration. Determined to leave no trace behind, Roz planned to carry these shells out of the camp and dispose of them responsibly. Amid their productive activities, the team recognized the importance of personal hygiene and self-care. Thankfully, the restroom facilities at the campsite were well-maintained, providing the team with the opportunity to freshen up and rejuvenate before embarking on their next thrilling trail.

The trip down from Blood Mountain was treacherous. With heavy backpacks pulling them forward, they had to maintain a backward stance to move forward, making it extremely difficult for the hikers. They paused briefly at

Flatrock Gap before tackling the Brandenburg Steps, the trail's steep, zigzagging descent. They say that this section is the hardest of the Georgia A.T. and the team again proved that to be true!

Just beyond the steps, a group of pheasants grazing near the trail startled Brian with their loud sound. They took off with such a loud noise while flying up beyond the canopy. Finally, below them, they could hear cars and trucks on the highway. They soon began seeing the vehicles through the trees and realized that they were close to the Walasi-Yi Center, where the Appalachian Trail (A.T.) passes right through the building. U.S. highway 29 and Georgia highway 129 were just below them, bustling with traffic. With renewed fervor, they made their way down the steep decline and reached the center.

11

Walasi-Yi Center

Inside, they found everything for the avid camper/backpacker. The Walasi-Yi Center served as a haven for hikers along the AT, offering an array of outdoor gear, camping equipment, and supplies. The shelves were stocked with high-quality tents, sleeping bags, backpacks, hiking boots, and all the essentials needed for a successful adventure on the Appalachian Trail. Hikers could find maps, guidebooks, and trail resources at the center to help them navigate the difficult terrain.

The bustling store attracted both experienced hikers and beginners alike. Excitement and anticipation filled the atmosphere as shoppers perused the aisles, marveling at the vast selection of gear. There were so many items on display, and they captivated Jake. His eyes lit up with each new discovery, and he couldn't help but imagine all the incredible adventures he could embark on with the gear in front of him. "I could just live here and be happy!" he thought.

The Walasi-Yi Center wasn't just a store, though. It was a gathering place for hikers to rest, recharge, and connect with fellow outdoor enthusiasts. The center had comfortable seating areas, a small cafe where hikers could enjoy a hot meal, and a friendly staff always ready to offer advice and share stories. It was a veritable oasis along the Appalachian Trail, providing much-needed support and resources for those undertaking the challenging journey.

As Brian and Jake explored the center, they couldn't help but feel a sense of excitement and camaraderie. They knew they had found a special place, one that would not only fulfill their hiking needs but also become a cherished memory of their Appalachian Trail experience.

Each team member felt it was a suitable time to get a hot snack in the cafe and to take out their cell phones and call home to let the folks know they were OK. Brian's mother, of course, wanted him to come home immediately after he had shared his adventure, but he told her he was going to stay with the group and that he was doing OK.

Mia's mother, who had been worried sick about her daughter, firmly voiced her insistence that they immediately return to Young Harris with no more delay. Concern and fear for her daughter's well-being were clear in her voice as she affectionately referred to Mia as "Babe." Despite understanding Mia's love for her friends, her mother passionately believed that it was time for Mia to call it quits, based on the troubling details Mia had previously shared about her experiences.

Jake called his dad, Mr. Sutton, to update him on their adventure. Mr. Sutton's tone of voice was noticeably different from Mia's mom. He expressed his excitement for them and acknowledged that he could have never expected the experiences they have had on the trip. Mr. Sutton encouraged Jake to stay strong and let the trail be their guide, assuring him that as long as they stayed on course, everything would be fine. Jake's dad also inquired about Roz, curious to know how she was handling the challenges of the trail. Jake replied with admiration, praising Roz for her invaluable nursing skills. He mentioned how she had been a godsend, providing the right medications and bandages for both him and Brian after their respective mishaps. Mr. Sutton responded with approval, acknowledging that Roz seemed like a keeper. Jake agreed, expressing how their bond had deepened significantly during the trip and how his love for her felt insurmountable.

Roz called home and got her little brother, Henry. "What's up, Sis?" Henry asked. "Bet you guys have had an exciting time up there. I'd love to have been with you, but you know mom would never have let me. Are you and

Jake doing good?" Roz responded to Henry, four years her junior, by telling him about some instances along the trail. She described the breathtaking views they encountered while hiking through the majestic mountains and shared stories of the wildlife they had spotted, including a family of deer and a soaring eagle. Henry listened intently; Roz's tales piqued his curiosity. He couldn't help but feel a pang of envy, wishing he could be there with them. Sensing his longing, Roz shared their next destination on the trail. "We're heading to Crystal Lake next," she revealed. "It's known for its clear waters and stunning surroundings. I wish you could join us, Henry. It would be so much fun." Henry's eyes widened with excitement as he imagined the beauty of Crystal Lake and the adventures that awaited Roz and Jake. "Wow! Sounds like a super fantastic trip, Roz. I'm envious and wish I could be there. Please take lots of pictures for me and tell me all about it when you get back."

Amid a challenging adventure, Roz's concern for her family remained unwavering. With a phone call to her little brother Henry, she sought reassurance that her mother was present. Little did she know that her mother's voice on the other end of the line would offer both comfort and admiration for Roz's bravery and resilience.

As Henry confirmed his mother's presence, Roz's heart

skipped a beat. Within seconds, her mother's soothing voice replaced Henry's on the phone. Concern laced every word as she asked, "How are you, dear?" Overwhelmed with relief, Roz reassured her mother that she was fine, despite the dangerous challenges she had faced on Black Mountain.

Eager to share her experiences, Roz recounted how she had used her nursing skills to aid her teammates, Brian, and Jake, who had suffered injuries along the treacherous trail. Her mother's voice trembled with worry upon learning about the narrow escape and daring rescue that Roz had been a part of. Yet, amidst the fear, her mother's pride shone through as she commended Roz for being the vital support the team needed during their time of crisis.

After the emotionally charged conversation, the team found solace in the simple pleasures of home. They called their loved ones and indulged in a hot snack in the cafe, replenishing their bodies and spirits. Energized by the unwavering support of their families, they embarked on the trail once more, their determination and enthusiasm renewed.

Roz's journey on Black Mountain was not just a test of physical endurance; it was a testament to the power of familial love and support. With her mother's unwavering belief in her strength and resilience, Roz found the courage to face the challenges that lay ahead. As she continued her adventure with her team, she carried the warmth of her family's encouragement, empowering her to be the helper and hero they knew she could be.

Jake, the team leader, made a quick decision when he realized that their original plan of reaching the Blue Mountain Shelter before nightfall would not happen. He scanned the surroundings and spotted a promising area that was level and free from excessive rocks. Wasting no time, he called out to the rest of the team, and they all agreed that this would be their campsite for the night. With a sense of urgency, they immediately got to work setting up their tents, carefully laying out their sleeping bags, and diligently collecting firewood. Jake and Brian, who had proven to be quite skilled in such situations, took charge of constructing a sturdy stone fire wall to contain the flames that would provide them with warmth and comfort throughout the challenging night ahead.

12

The Hand of Fate

Exploring the grassy hillside, the diverse array of plants she encountered captivated Mia, many of which were entirely unfamiliar to her. Intrigued by their beauty, she carefully plucked leaves and flowers, preserving them as pressed specimens in her cherished book of memories. However, the idyllic camping experience took an unexpected turn when nature called, and the absence of facilities necessitated finding suitable spots for personal relief. In a stroke of unfortunate luck, the adventurous Jake unknowingly positioned himself near a large rhododendron that housed a furious hornet's nest.

With each sting inflicting painful jolts, he hurriedly retreated to the safety of the camp. Fortunately, quick-thinking Roz had packed aloe cream in her backpack, which she promptly applied to each welt, providing much-needed relief for Jake's suffering. Throughout the night, Jake's condition worsened as he developed a fever that disrupted his sleep. Yet Roz, an ever-dependable nurse, remained by his side, applying additional aloe cream to ease his discomfort and offer solace during the restless night.

Roz had given Jake Tylenol for his fever, and it seemed to work around midnight when his fever finally broke.

In the darkness of early morning, thunder rumbled, waking team members with its ominous warning of impending rain. The wind whirled about their small tents. Before long, the heavens opened, and the team experienced a very terrifying thunderstorm. They saw lightning strikes through the tent walls, and they were afraid. The storm quickly became reminiscent of the Gooch Gap storm a few nights before.

As the storm rages on, a loud, crackling noise echoes through the forest. An ancient oak tree tilts and falls, its massive trunk plunging toward the campsite. Brian, distracted by securing the tent, barely has time to react. The ground shakes as the tree crashes down, landing on Brian. The team rushes out of their tents in the driving rain and can see Brian underneath the tree. Mia, realizing the seriousness of the moment and their inability to remove the large tree from Brian, caresses Brian's face when he utters his last words: "I ... love ... you."

Oh, where does the love of God go in a moment like

that? How does one contend with the most tragic moment of your life? Seeing your dear friend and beloved
fiancé, Brian, lying there beneath that behemoth of a tree,
crushed by its weight, with no way to rescue him this
time, an overwhelming sense of despair sets in. The once
vibrant forest now feels hauntingly silent, as if even nature
mourns the loss. In this heart-wrenching moment, where
does one turn for solace and strength? How does one find
the courage to face the unimaginable reality that Brian is
gone forever?

Quickly, Jake told the two girls, Mia and Roz, to stay
with their injured friend, Brian, while he ventured back
down the treacherous trail to the Walasi-Yi Center for
help. The rain poured down relentlessly, creating a curtain
of water that made visibility almost impossible. Lightning strikes illuminated the dark sky, adding an extra layer of danger to the already challenging situation. Undeterred by the inclement weather, Jake mustered every
ounce of strength and determination as he embarked on
his mission to save his dear friend, Brian. Moving at a
brisk pace, adrenaline coursing through his veins, Jake battled against the slippery and muddy terrain, slipping, and
falling several times. However, his unwavering focus on
Brian's well-being propelled him forward. Thoughts of his
friend, lying injured and vulnerable, were the only thing

occupying Jake's mind as he fervently prayed to God, desperately hoping for a miraculous intervention. With each step, the distance between Jake and the Walasi-Yi Center seemed to shrink, fueling his determination to get help as quickly as possible.

At the Center, a recreational facility nestled deep in the heart of the mountains, Jake found himself in a distressing situation. He had rushed to the center in a panic, desperate for help. Jake's urgent pounding on the front door roused the store owner, Mr. Rogers his slumber. Mr. Rogers, sensing the urgency in Jake's voice, wasted no time in allowing him inside.

Once inside, the gravity of the situation became apparent. Jake explained that a massive tree had come crashing down on his friend Brian, trapping him underneath. The shock of the news prompted Mr. Rogers to take immediate action. He dialed the emergency services and requested an ambulance and a Civil Defense crew to be dispatched to the scene.

As Mr. Rogers relayed the plan of action to Jake, the reality of the situation slowly sank in. The rescue team would have to navigate a treacherous two-mile trail up the mountainside to reach Brian, and then another two miles back down, all while contending with the obstacle of the fallen tree. The enormity of the task weighed heavily on

Jake, and he crumbled under the weight of his emotions.

Overwhelmed with grief and fear, Jake found solace in the comforting presence of Mrs. Rogers, who emerged from their quarters wearing a hastily thrown on nightgown. She tenderly consoled Jake, offering whatever support she could in this trying moment. The Center for Outdoor Adventure, known for its camaraderie and sense of community, was now a place of shared sorrow and hope, as everyone rallied together in the face of adversity.

Mr. Rogers, the experienced guide at the Center, reassured Jake that help was on the way after he had contacted Search and Rescue and the local ambulance service. However, he informed Jake that it would take an hour for them to arrive at their location and then hike up the two miles. Faced with the prospect of waiting for help, Jake expressed his urgency to return to his friends, who were still out on the trail. Understanding Jake's predicament, Mr. Rogers empathized with him and reluctantly granted permission for him to brave the treacherous weather and make his way back uphill. Concerned for Jake's safety, Mr. Rogers expressed his heartfelt apologies for the unfortunate circumstances he found himself in and acknowledged the grim reality that accidents, sometimes even fatal, can occur in such unpredictable situations.

Roz, a student nurse, immediately sprang into action

when she checked Brian's pulse and found none. With a heavy heart, she turned to Mia and delivered the devastating news: Brian was no longer with them. Their world suddenly shattered, but Roz knew they had to gather their strength and support each other in this unimaginable time of grief. Jake, their trusted friend, would be returning soon, and they needed to be prepared to share the heartbreaking news with him.

As the minutes dragged on, Mia and Roz began the somber task of taking down a nearby tent. With great care, they covered Brian's lifeless body, shielding him from the elements and giving him a dignified farewell. The two women then crawled underneath the tent, seeking solace and comfort as they mourned the loss of their dear friend. Their embrace of one another was intense and lasted until they heard Jake's voice calling out in the darkness.

In moments like these, time seems to stretch endlessly, each tick of the clock a painful reminder of the void left behind. It is a stark contrast to the fleeting moments of joy and happiness when time seems to slip through our fingers, leaving us craving for more.

As Jake entered the camp and crawled under the tent to find Mia and Roz, he informed them about the actions he had taken. He explained he had awakened the owner of the Center, Mr. Rogers, who had immediately called for a Search and Rescue team and an ambulance. However, he mentioned it would take an hour for them to reach the Center, considering the distance and the rugged terrain of the mountain. Jake also emphasized that the actual time it would take for the team to make their way up the mountain was uncertain. The three embraced for what seemed an eternity while awaiting the desperate help they needed. Wet, cold, and alone on the mountainside, the three commiserated together.

It would be two hours later before a team reached them and began the arduous task of removing the section of tree around Brian with chainsaws. There were eight men, two with the ambulance service, and six from Search and Rescue. The men battled the persistent rainstorm until they freed Brian.

Brian's call to his mom yesterday came to mind for Jake, and he wondered who should call her to relay the news. She had told Brian then to come home after he had shared the terrifying details of his near fatality on Black Mountain. Jake couldn't imagine how she must be feeling, hearing about her son's close brush with death. Mia, sensing the urgency and the emotional toll it would take on Brian's mom, selflessly offered to make the call once they reached the Center. The ambulance crew had advised the three of them to return to the Center and get warm and dry, as they knew the rescue mission would be time-consuming. The process of safely bringing Brian's body down the treacherous hillside would be an arduous and lengthy one.

When they returned to the Walasi-Yi Center, Mr. and Mrs. Rogers greeted them with hugs and had a fresh pot of coffee made. There was also a deputy sheriff there to take their statements about the accident.

At 8 a.m., Mia called Mrs. Foster, Brian's mom. She answered the phone and immediately asked, "Is Brian O.K.? I had a bad dream about him last night, especially after he told me about his incident on Black Mountain." As Mia listened to her recount her dream, Mrs. Branson soon asked, "Mia, why are you calling me at this time of the morning?"

Mia then unraveled the horrifying story and Brian's death. All night long, the team had been trying feverishly to get help and get Brian off the mountainside. Finally, a team of search and rescue people were up the mountain cutting away the tree and freeing Brian so they could bring him down to the Center.

Mr. Foster, a farmer in Telfair County, Georgia, took the phone from his wife, and Mia had to recount the story all over again, sobbing unrelentingly. Paul Foster asked Mia about the others. "Are you O.K., Mia, and what about Jake and Roz? How are they doing?"

Mr. Foster, they're doing all they can. The awful rainstorm last night drenched us completely. It was the continuous downpours, we suspect, that brought the tree down. That old tree was precariously situated. Please accept our deepest condolences for your loss; we'll support you, especially during Brian's funeral.

Mr. Foster was crying on the other end and trying to console Mrs. Foster. Mia, their close family friend, could hear their heart-wrenching sobs and felt an overwhelming urge to offer her help and support. Despite her own grief, Mia mustered up the strength to speak, letting Mr. Foster know she was there for them. In between sobs, Mr. Foster thanked Mia for her kindness, but insisted that they would take it from there. However, Mia couldn't bear the thought of them having to handle everything alone. Determined to ease some of their burden, she gently reminded Mr. Foster that the funeral home in Blairsville, Georgia, could assist with the arrangements for bringing Brian's body home. She assured him he could call the funeral home to discuss the details and ensure Brian received the utmost respect and care.

This harrowing experience solidifies their resolve to leave the trail and head for home, grateful for the adventure but wise enough to walk away while they still can.

The rain eases as the morning lingered. Two men carried Brian's body down the mountain and put it in the back of an ambulance. Jake then called Amicalola to ask if someone could come to the Center and pick them up. He would gladly pay them whatever it cost. Knowing what had just happened, the director at Amicalola Falls State Park assured Jake that they would have a van to pick them up in about an hour or so.

The van driver, a burly looking middle-aged man, would drive the team back to Amicalola to pick up Jake's truck. He asks about the night before. "What happened to you guys up there? I was told that someone died. Is that true?"

Jake related the story of the harrowing night to Francis, the driver, and talked about Brian's death, the terrible storm, and the aftermath of the rescue. The van descended Blood Mountain, turned at the crossing at Turner's Grocery Store, made it over to Highway 60, and then to Dahlonega. In Dahlonega, the van turned west towards Amicalola, arriving shortly thereafter.

Tired, weary, and broken-hearted to have left poor Brian in the back of that ambulance, weighed heavily upon their minds as they loaded their equipment into Jake's Ford F-150 and headed back to Young Harris. It would be a sad and long day ahead for the weary team, not one less.

Mia, with tears welling up in her eyes, started the conversation in their drive back, acknowledging the divine intervention that had saved them. She thanked God for guiding them through the treacherous storm that had tested their resilience and faith. She also asked the team to be in much prayer for Brian's family and the days ahead. The three talked about planning to attend his funeral service down in Helena, Georgia, and they all agreed to make it happen.

Surviving the storm and narrowly avoiding tragedy had brought Mia, Roz, and Jake even closer together. This shared experience served as a reminder of the fragility of life and the importance of cherishing every moment. It was a muted trip back to Young Harris. Mia soon fell asleep in the back seat while Roz and Jake softly whispered conversations in the front.

13

Saying Farewell to Brian

Morning broke for the three friends, Mia, Roz, and Jake, as they awakened to a luscious warm day at Young Harris. However, their preparations for Brian's funeral in Helena, Georgia, five hours away, cast a somber tone over the day. With heavy hearts, they left their college campus around 7 a.m. and embarked on the journey in Mia's trusty Toyota Camry, determined to reach their destination as quickly as possible.

As they drove through the picturesque countryside, the friends couldn't help but reflect on the memories they had shared with Brian. Brian's love of farming endeared him to the team. His sudden departure had shaken their tight-knit group, leaving them with a deep sense of loss and sadness. Helena, a place unknown to them until now, awaited their arrival with a mix of curiosity and trepidation.

Upon reaching Helena, they discovered a town that exuded a quaint charm, despite the grief that hung in the air. As they navigated through the muted streets, they noticed a solemn atmosphere, with cars lining the roads around Lowe's Funeral Home. The parking lot behind the building was already overflowing with vehicles, a testament to the impact Brian had on the community.

Finding their way to the funeral home on Main Street, the trio joined the gathering crowd, their presence a small tribute to their dear friend. Beautiful flowers adorned the room inside, which was filled with hushed voices and tearful embraces. Brian's loved ones, friends, and acquaintances had come together to honor his life and offer support to one another during this grim time.

As Mia, Jake, Roz, and the rest of the mourners gathered to say their last goodbyes, they couldn't help but feel a mix of sorrow and gratitude. Sorrow for losing their beloved friend, but gratitude for the opportunity to celebrate the impact he had made on their lives and the lives of so many others.

Entering the room with Brian's body, Mia ran to Mrs. Foster, and they held an endless hug with each other and both began crying. Jake and Roz greeted Mr. Foster and the rest of the family, but Mia could not bring herself to leave Mrs. Foster. A bond had developed between the two since Mia had been so close to Mrs. Foster's son for the past three years.

Mia then noticed the casket, a simple wooden one, so beautifully detailed in every way. She walked over to Brian with Mrs. Foster. Mia could not contain herself. She bent over the casket and hugged Brian's lifeless body, and the tears flowed.

Jake and the team sat with the Foster family for about an hour, and then it was time for the service at First Baptist Church in the neighboring town of McRae. Mrs. Foster had requested that the team sit with the family members at the church.

The procession to the church was about a one-mile drive from the funeral home. McRae and Helena have always shared back-to-back city signs with each other. Despite the mile-long trip, it took forever to get all the cars lined up and parked. The Foster family was immensely popular in the area, so people came from near and far to the service.

Inside the old historical church, Jake, Mia, and Roz found every pew filled to a standing room only. The family sat in the reserved seats down front.

The Fosters had asked Brian's best friend, Jake Sutton, to give the eulogy while the minister offered prayers and scripture readings, so Jake sat with the minister down on the platform.

The service was beautiful in every aspect and handled

well by Lowe's funeral home. When it became time for Jake's eulogy, a young friend of Brian's stood to sing "Amazing Grace" in his honor.

Jake stood, unsure of himself, but knew that Brian was counting on him.

JAKE'S EULOGY:

Ladies and Gentlemen, friends and loved ones,

We gather here today to remember and honor the life of a remarkable individual, Brian Foster. It is with a heavy heart that I stand before you, tasked with the tough duty of delivering this eulogy for a man whose presence and spirit brought joy, strength, and inspiration to all who knew him.

Brian was many things: a devoted friend, a loving family member, an adventurous soul, and a beacon of kindness. The qualities we all admired—his unwavering determination, his generosity, and his ability to find beauty in the simplest moments—marked his life.

As I reflect on Brian's life, I am reminded of the many moments we shared on the Appalachian Trail. He embraced every challenge and reveled in the journey, finding solace in nature's embrace. Our time on the trail was not just about the miles hiked, but about the bonds formed, the stories shared, and the memories created.

Brian often spoke about life and death with a wisdom

that belied his years. He saw life as a journey, a precious gift to be cherished and lived to its fullest. He believed that every moment, whether filled with joy or sorrow, was a part of the grand tapestry of our existence. To Brian, death was not an end but a transition—a part of the natural cycle that united all living things.

His philosophy was simple yet profound: live with purpose, love without restraint, and embrace the unknown with courage. He found comfort because our lives, though finite, have the power to leave an everlasting impact through the connections we make and the love we share.

Brian's untimely departure is a profound loss, and all who had the privilege of knowing him will feel deeply the pain of his absence. Yet, in mourning, we also celebrate the legacy he leaves behind. We take solace in knowing that Brian lived fully, with passion and purpose, and his spirit will continue to inspire us.

Let us remember Brian not for how he left us, but for how he lived—bravely, kindly, and with a heart full of love. May his memory be a guiding star, lighting the path for us as we continue our journey, cherishing the moments we have and the people we hold dear.

Rest in peace, Brian. We will dearly miss you, but never forget you. On behalf of your classmates at Young Harris, we love you, Brian.

The five-hour drive back to Young Harris seemed endless. Jake and Roz, city slickers, had never seen so many crops growing along the highways. When they finally reached Interstate 16, they took a stop in Macon to eat an early evening dinner at a Waffle House.

Reaching Young Harris around 10 p.m., the three separated for the evening. The days ahead would be tough, but their spirits would be strong. They faced the future now without Brian, but each would honor him in their hearts. "There, but by the Grace of God, go you and I."

14

The Uganda Project

Sarah and Mia graduated from UGA in May 1982. Filled with a sense of purpose and adventure, they embarked on a life-changing journey by joining the Uganda Project, a humanitarian initiative aimed at improving the lives of the local population in Uganda. For Mia, this trip held an even deeper significance as it brought back memories of Brian, her late partner, and their shared dreams of making a difference in Uganda and embarking on an epic Appalachian Trail Trip together.

Before she could leave, however, Mia had one important event to attend: the wedding of her friends, Jake and Roz. Not only was she invited to the wedding, but she also had the honor of being Roz's bridesmaid. Determined to make it to the wedding and still catch her flight, Mia carefully planned her schedule. She knew she had just enough time to make it to the wedding in Roswell, return to Athens, pack her bags, and meet her friend Sarah at the airport in

Atlanta. Luckily, the drive from Athens to Roswell was short, taking only about an hour and a half. Mia arrived at Jake's home in Roswell, where she would stay for the two days surrounding the wedding. On the night of the wedding, they held the reception at the charming Red Barn in the picturesque countryside just ten miles north of Roswell. The joy and excitement of Jake and the Sutton family were palpable as they welcomed Mia. Jake and the Sutton family were thrilled at having Mia at the wedding, feeling as if Christmas had come early. Jake assured Mia that Roz would arrive in about an hour, and she would go over all the details with her then.

Roz had the most elaborate wedding the State of Georgia has ever had! It was a grand affair, filled with opulence and extravagance that left everyone in awe. The wedding planners meticulously planned the event, overlooking no detail. To create a magical atmosphere, they meticulously chose every detail, from the breathtaking venue to the exquisite decorations. The night before the wedding, they held the rehearsal and dinner at the Barn, a charming rustic venue adorned with twinkling lights and beautiful floral arrangements. Anticipation and excitement filled Mia as she arrived at the rehearsal. Little did she know, a heartwarming surprise awaited her. Jake, the groom, had left a space open beside him at the head table in honor of

Brian, his best man, and Mia's late fiancé. It was a touching gesture that brought tears to Mia's eyes and filled her heart with gratitude. The wedding weekend was truly a celebration of love, friendship, and cherished memories.

The passage of time had inevitably altered Mia's perspective, and she now viewed this opportunity as one of many incredible experiences in her life. She couldn't help but reflect on the whispers of fate that guided her from one place to another, leading her to Uganda. Embracing this new chapter, Mia wholeheartedly threw herself into the Uganda Project, immersing herself in the daily chores, embracing the local culture, and dedicating her efforts to the memory of Brian.

Although Brian had initially planned to accompany Mia on this journey, his premature death had left her with only his spirit to guide her. Mia channeled her grief into her work, pouring her heart and soul into her mission in Uganda. Over the next four years of her contract, she made remarkable progress in her projects, leaving a lasting impact on the community she served.

Mia's dedication to the Uganda Project not only honored Brian's memory but also allowed her to find renewed excitement and purpose in her life. She discovered a profound sense of fulfillment in her service, knowing that she was making a difference in the lives of those she encountered. With each passing day, Mia's journey continued to unfold, taking her to unexpected places and shaping her into the person she would be.

In April 1986, Mia received a life-changing phone call from her favorite professor at the University of Georgia (UGA). The offer was an exciting one—a teaching position in horticulture. Without hesitating, Mia immediately accepted the offer. Mia had been living in Uganda, where she had experienced significant weight loss because of poor dieting and limited access to nutritious food and clean water. She saw this opportunity to return home as a chance to "fatten up," as she humorously referred to it. The prospect of teaching the skills she had gained during her time in Uganda back in her hometown was exhilarating. Saying her farewell to the villagers she had grown close to and bidding goodbye to her friend Sarah, Mia embarked on her journey back to Athens, Georgia, in May. Little did she know that this would be her new home for an indefinite period.

Mia, a new faculty member at UGA, wasted no time in securing an apartment that perfectly suited her needs. A charming two-bedroom townhouse near the bustling campus became Mia's new home, and she was thrilled. With its cozy atmosphere and convenient location, she felt an instant sense of belonging. Mia arrived just in time, settling in days before the summer semester started. Her contract assigned Mia to teach three classes during the upcoming summer session, a prospect that excited her immensely. Eager to make a lasting impact on her students, she eagerly awaited the opportunity to share her knowledge and expertise in the classroom. With her new apartment serving as a haven of comfort and inspiration, Mia felt confident that she was well-prepared for the exciting journey that lay ahead.

Mia would soon meet Billy Hinton from Cartersville, Georgia, and they began dating in the fall of 1986. She was hesitant at first to meet someone new, but she felt as though she needed to move on in her life. Brian would want that. Billy taught in the science department at Georgia, so it seemed a match made in heaven.

Two years later, Mia and Billy would be wed in Mia's hometown of Silver Springs, Florida. It was not a very elaborate affair, but only a few close friends and family members in attendance. Roz would make the trip down with Jake. Roz would be Mia's bridesmaid.

15

Back to Friendly Surroundings

Jake and the team of three now, comprising Mia, and Roz, took a couple of days to recoup from their previous endeavors and Brian's funeral. They had just successfully organized a charity event that raised funds for a local shelter that would be named in honor of Brian and his faithful work. It would be lovingly called "Brian's Shelter" and would have a plaque at the front entrance that told the story of Brian's premature death on the A.T. With a sense of accomplishment, they began talking about their next major event, which was none other than their upcoming graduation in May. Realizing that there were only three weeks left before finals and the big day, each member of the team buckled down and devoted themselves to intense studying to prepare for their exams.

To recharge her batteries before diving into the last

stretch at Young Harris, Mia took a trip home during the remaining days of spring break. She longed to spend quality time with family and friends, eager for a temporary escape from the pressures of academia. Jake and Roz made the conscious decision to remain on campus. They believed that the quiet campus atmosphere would provide them with an optimal environment for studying and concentration. With determination in their hearts, the team embraced this brief period of separation, knowing that they would reunite soon to celebrate their achievements and bid farewell to their beloved college years at Young Harris.

The vibrant energy of spring greeted Mia when she returned to her university campus after a few days at home with family. Blooming flowers and lush green trees transformed the campus into a picturesque scene. Fresh blossoms filled the air with their sweet scent, and birds chirping added a symphony of nature to the atmosphere. The students were delighted to see their friends again as they all gathered on the quad, basking in the warm sunshine. The campus was abuzz with activity, with students playing frisbee, studying under the shade of trees, and enjoying outdoor picnics. It was as if the entire campus had transformed into a vibrant oasis, offering a respite from the dreary winter months. Spring had truly arrived, and Mia couldn't help but feel a renewed sense of excitement and joy as she embarked on the rest of the semester filled with possibilities AND graduation!

Now, only three friends—Mia, Jake, and Roz—gathered at the quad and enjoyed a bittersweet picnic, prepared with love and care by Mia and Roz. The sun was shining, casting a warm glow over the picturesque surroundings. Mia had packed a delicious assortment of sandwiches, fruit salads, and homemade cookies, while Roz had brought along a refreshing cooler filled with an assortment of beverages. While enjoying a delicious meal and each other's company on the soft grass, their conversation eventually turned to a topic they'd been pondering—"the trail." And, of course, the death of their dear friend, Brian.

The trail had become somewhat of a legend in Young Harris. It was renowned for its breathtaking views, winding through lush forests, cascading waterfalls, and rugged cliffs. Despite its difficulty, the trail's rewards made for a thrilling experience for those who dared to hike it.

Jake, always up for an adventure, listened intently as Mia described the steep climbs, narrow paths, and the feeling of accomplishment that awaited at the trail's summit. Jake seemed skeptical about the whole endeavor, complaining about his lack of leadership. However, Roz, who had a knack for encouraging her friends, reassured Jake that they supported him as their fearless leader throughout the hike. Jake felt like he should have done something to save Brian, but Mia and Roz assured him there was nothing he could have done.

As they talked about "the trail," grief hung heavy in the air. Each recalled the trail with a mixture of joyful and fearful memories.

Roz then spoke about Brian's remarkable abilities in escaping many disasters along the treacherous trail. She recounted how Brian, with his unwavering determination and quick thinking, had evaded countless life-threatening situations. Brian's survival of a Black Mountain fall and a bear attack convinced Roz that Mother Nature was targeting him. Her fury was unrelenting, throwing one calamity after another in Brian's path. Yet, against all odds, he had emerged victorious repeatedly, defying the forces of nature with his sheer resilience until the disaster that fateful night when the ancient oak tree had fallen upon him during that heavy downpour and thunderstorm.

Jake, the spirited and adventurous member of the team, eagerly interjected into the conversation, demanding some recognition for his own accomplishments. With a mischievous grin, he reminded his teammates of the daring challenges he had conquered during their expedition. Not only had he bravely survived Brian's daring rescue mission, but he had also faced a relentless hornet attack with unwavering courage. As his words hung in the air, the team members couldn't help but burst into laughter, appreciating Jake's carefree and lighthearted outlook on their unforgettable trip.

As the picnic wound down, the friends headed back to their dorms to study for their final exams. With their final Young Harris exams only days off, they aimed for thorough preparation.

The following week, Mia was called to the Dean's Office. As she entered his room, Dean Jones began telling her about her outstanding services to the community and how much she and her friends had done for the Young Harris campus. He had admired her studies and abilities since she first arrived on campus and wanted Mia to know that her top grades earned her the class Valedictorian position!

Mia was beside herself with excitement and disbelief when she found out that her scores were tops on the entire campus. She had been working tirelessly, studying day and night, but never did she imagine she would outperform everyone else. It was a moment of pure joy and pride for Mia. However, amidst her jubilation, a pang of guilt crept into her heart as she thought about her close friend, Becky Simpson. Mia knew Becky had always been an excellent student, often achieving high scores just like her. She couldn't help but feel a sense of sadness, knowing that Becky had set her sights on becoming the Valedictorian of their graduating class. Mia dreaded the thought of breaking the news to her friend, fearing that it would shatter Becky's dreams and dampen their friendship. After learning that Becky would be the Salutatorian, Mia felt relieved. She and Becky would sit together on the platform the day of graduation and Mia would give her Valedictorian speech. She really didn't know where she would begin in manufacturing that speech but knew that she had ample help from her friends, Jake, and Roz.

When she broke the news to the team, they were exuberant, filled with joy for Mia. They knew that she was the best student on campus and her award merely confirmed it. That night, the team took her over to Blairsville for an enjoyable meal together at the Texas Roadhouse. Steaks, baked potatoes, and all the trimmings were paid for by Jake in tribute to Brian, their dear friend, and Mia. Mia was again very humble and thankful that these people whom she admired had taken this time to congratulate her on her achievement. Jake spoke up, "Mia, I know that you are graduating Summa Cum Laude, but I'll be graduating with *Thank You, Laude*!" The team had a good laugh at the always funny Jake Sutton and his remark.

At the end of the meal, Jake had the kitchen crew bring

out a molten lava cake in honor of Mia's achievement. Mia was so appreciative for the goodheartedness of her friends and their camaraderie.

Graduation day soon arrived, and the parents of Jake, Mia and Roz, felt excitement and anticipation. They had been looking forward to this moment for years, eagerly awaiting the culmination of their children's hard work and dedication. The proud parents had made all the arrangements to be present on this special day. Some had driven up the evening before, ensuring they were well-rested and ready to witness their child's achievement. Most of them had rented comfortable rooms in the neighboring town of Blue Ridge, where they could relax and prepare for the festivities.

However, Mia's family had rented a room in Young Harris, a decision made intending to spend a memorable evening with their daughter before the big day. As the morning of graduation dawned, the four friends and their families gathered at the quad, their hearts full of love and support for one another. They exchanged warm embraces, cherishing this last moment of togetherness before the grand celebration. The parents, dressed in their finest attire, exuded elegance, and pride as they mingled with one another. Suits, ties, evening gowns, and other formal garments adorned their figures, reflecting the significance of the occasion. Nervous excitement and joyful anticipation filled the air as the families prepared to witness their children's educational journey culminating, at least for now. All the team would continue their studies at other universities over the next two years.

When it became time for Mia to give her commencement address as Valedictorian, she was in tears and wasn't sure if she could make it through the speech. As she looked out upon the crowd, she quickly noticed the smiling faces of Jake and Roz and remembered their Appalachian Trail trip. Thoughts of the trip were swimming in her head; each momentous event, each step up and down the trail, the rainstorms and the Brian's death. And then she looked at her parents, filled with pride in their little girl and her accomplishments, and her heart filled at that point with an overwhelming compassion.

The college president, Dr. Paul Specter stood and addressed the crowd.

The esteemed Dean of Students, Dr. Edwin Jones, a well-respected figure at our university, tells me that after carefully evaluating academic achievements, he has completed the calculations. It is with immense pleasure and excitement that I announce the selection of Mia Spencer as the Valedictorian of the class of 1980. Mia's exceptional dedication, unparalleled intellect, and unwavering commitment to excellence have earned her this prestigious title. Her remarkable academic prowess is further highlighted by her forthcoming graduation with all honors and the highest distinction of Summa Cum Laude. The entire university community takes immense pride in Mia and her outstanding accomplishments. Mia's exceptional abilities and unwavering determination will allow her to make a lasting impact on the world. Therefore, I now invite Mia Strawbridge to step forward and deliver her valedictory address, as she leads us forward into the future with her inspiring words. With that, Mia stood and made her way to the podium, shaking hands with Dr. Spencer.

With both legs trembling, her hands shaking her notes, and her heart filled with determination, Mia stood there addressing the crowd on that gorgeous spring day in May 1980. In the bustling college square, colorful blooming flowers and the college buildings surrounding the event all formed a stunning backdrop. The crowd eagerly gathered, their faces reflecting anticipation and curiosity as they waited to hear what Mia had to say. They set the stage with a microphone, amplifying Mia's voice to reach every corner of the square. As she took a deep breath, Mia glanced at her carefully prepared notes, superbly written on yellowed pages that held countless hours of research and dedication. The sun gently kissed her face, casting a warm glow that brought out the determination in her eyes.

Mia's speech was not just any ordinary address; it was a pivotal moment in her life, a culmination of years of arduous work and a testament to her unwavering commitment to a cause she believed in. The crowd comprised people from all social classes - young and old, men and women, representing diverse cultures and backgrounds. A common desire for change united them, and they looked at Mia to provide the guidance and inspiration they sought.

As Mia spoke, her voice quivered slightly, but her words carried a weight that resonated with each listener. She spoke passionately about the injustices she had witnessed; the struggles faced by marginalized communities, and the urgent need for equality and compassion. Mia carefully chose her words, each sentence delivering a powerful message that resonated with the audience.

The crowd remained silent, captivated by Mia's presence and the sincerity that radiated from her every word. They hung on to her every syllable, feeling a surge of hope and determination building within them. Mia's trembling legs gradually gained strength as her hands steadied, and her notes became a mere guide rather than a crutch. She was no longer just an individual standing on a stage; she had become a voice, a symbol of resilience and determination.

Friends, faculty, and fellow graduates of the Class of 1980,

It is an honor to stand before you today as we celebrate this incredible milestone. Today, we not only commemorate our academic achievements, but also reflect on the journeys that have shaped us into who we are.

Graduating with honors is a testament to our dedication, perseverance, and unwavering pursuit of excellence. Each one of us has faced unique challenges and obstacles along the way, but we've emerged stronger and more resilient because of them. Together, we've grown, supported one another, and shared countless memories that will last a lifetime.

Our time at Young Harris brought us many moments of discovery, learning, and growth. Challenges pushed us to think critically, question the world, and push our potential boundaries. We've forged friendships and connections that have enriched our lives and will continue to do so.

I'd like to take a moment to share a personal experience that underscores the importance of resilience and the power of the human spirit. Recently, my friends and I embarked on a journey along the Appalachian Trail—a place where the whispering trees and the rhythm of our footsteps connected us to something greater than ourselves.

We faced harsh weather, difficult terrain, and moments that tested our limits. One night, under a canopy of ancient stars and with the mountain mists closing in, we encountered a tragedy that reminded us of our vulnerabilities. The storm brought down a huge tree that tragically crushed and killed my fiancé and best friend. It was a terrifying and humbling experience that made us realize the true strength of our bond and the importance of knowing when to prioritize our safety. The trail, with its hidden dangers and serene beauty, taught us about the delicate balance between bravery and caution.

Returning to the trailhead, we felt a profound sense of gratitude—not just for our safety, but for the lessons the trail had imparted. It taught us to listen not only to the echoes of nature but also to our inner voices, guiding us with wisdom and insight. It taught us to treasure every moment and every experience with one another, for death is always imminent. I know that all too well. You see, there is someone who was very dear to me who lost his life on the trail. Brian, I feel your presence with us now.

As we stand here today, on the brink of fresh adventures and opportunities, let us carry forward the mystique of the trail and the lessons we've learned. Let us embrace the challenges ahead with determination and resilience. Let us support one another and cherish the bonds we've formed.

And let us never forget that our strength lies not only in our individual accomplishments, but also in our collective spirit.

To the Class of 1980, congratulations! May you continue to strive for greatness, seek knowledge, and make a positive impact on the world. Your journey is just beginning, and I know that each of you will achieve remarkable things.

Thank you, and best of luck to all of you in your future endeavors. May God bless you.

As Mia concluded her speech, the crowd erupted into thunderous applause, their hands clapping in unison and their cheers filling the air. Mia's heart swelled with a sense of accomplishment and fulfillment, knowing that she had impacted the lives of those who had listened to her. The gorgeous spring day in May 1980, marked a turning point not only in Mia's journey but also in the hearts and minds of the people who had witnessed her powerful address.

And that would be the last time that the three would be together as a team. Their journey together had ended, and the trail of a lifetime was only beginning.

Jake, Brian, Mia, and Roz embarked on an incredible journey together, exploring the breathtaking wonders of the Appalachian Trail. Their bond grew stronger as they faced the challenges and marvels of nature, forging unforgettable memories along the way. Four great friends went on the trail; only three came out!

After completing the trail, they each pursued their dreams at different universities. Jake chose Georgia Tech, where he dedicated himself to earning a P.E. (Professional Engineering) degree, determined to excel in his chosen field. Meanwhile, Mia found her place at the University of Georgia in Athens, immersing themselves in the vibrant academic and social atmosphere of the campus. Roz continued her educational journey at South University in Atlanta, pursuing a master's degree in nursing, driven by her passion for healthcare and helping others.

Although occasional phone calls maintained their connection, they could never again experience the closeness of their epic adventure. The Appalachian Trail, with its perilous obstacles, breathtaking vistas, and timeless wildlife, would forever hold a special place in their hearts as they ventured onward to conquer new horizons and fulfill their aspirations for the future.

Still, while each would lie on their beds, they could hear the voices calling. They could vividly see Mishipeshu down by the water, coming in and out, and the eerie sounds would reverberate in their heads. The tall ancient trees of the trail would beckon them, and the whispers never ceased. And now, whispers of their dear friend Brian would echo through those hallowed hills.

16

New Beginnings

Where one trail in life ends, another begins. This simple yet profound statement encapsulates the essence of our journey through life. Life is a series of interconnected paths, each leading to new experiences, opportunities, and challenges. Just as we reach the end of one trail, we stand at the threshold of another, ready to embark on a new adventure. These trails may be literal, like the hiking trails that wind through majestic mountains or meander along tranquil beaches. They may also be metaphorical, representing the different stages and transitions we encounter in our personal and professional lives.

Regardless of the form they take, these trails serve as markers of progress, guiding us towards personal growth, self-discovery, and fulfillment. They encourage us to embrace change, to step out of our comfort zones, and to embrace the unknown. Navigating these trails constantly challenges us to adapt, learn, and evolve.

Each new trail presents an opportunity for us to explore uncharted territories, to broaden our horizons, and to discover hidden talents and passions. Along the way, we may encounter obstacles and setbacks, but it is through these challenges that we grow stronger and more resilient. With each trail, we gain valuable experiences, insights, and memories that shape us into the individuals we are today. So, as one trail ends, let must embrace the beginning of another with open hearts and open minds, ready to embrace the adventures that lie ahead.

Jake Sutton, always the fearless adventurer, was enjoying his spring break in Fort Lauderdale, Florida, alongside his friends from Georgia Tech. Their thrilling escapades took an unexpected turn when they were involved in a harrowing car accident, narrowly escaping a fatal outcome. Unfortunately, Jake bore the brunt of the impact and found himself confined to a hospital bed, nursing various scrapes and contusions. In addition, he suffered a concussion, necessitating several days of close observation and medical care.

Thankfully, his companions emerged from the accident unscathed, albeit shaken by the traumatic experience. With George's car rendered undrivable, they had no choice but to rent a vehicle to make the journey back to Atlanta, leaving Jake behind in the hospital. However, Roz, upon receiving the distressing news, immediately made her way to Fort Lauderdale to support Jake during his recovery. She provided him with the utmost care and attention, ensuring his comfort and well-being. When the time came for their return to Georgia, Roz took it upon herself to accompany Jake and safely transport him back to Georgia Tech, where he would resume his studies.

Roz, the insatiable wedding planner, discussed the details of their upcoming wedding on her birthday the following year while they drove back to Atlanta. As they delved into the various aspects of the event, Jake suddenly proposed the idea of eloping, perhaps to avoid the stress and overwhelming nature of a traditional wedding. However, Roz couldn't hide her immediate distaste for his suggestion. With a hint of disappointment in her voice, she firmly informed Jake that their wedding was going to be a grand affair, held at the exquisite Fincher's Barn, complete with all the extravagant fanfare that befits such a momentous occasion.

An elaborate country wedding to Roz is a celebration of love and nature that combines rustic charm with sophisticated elegance. Set in the breathtaking countryside, this wedding is a feast for the senses. The venue is a picturesque barn adorned with twinkling fairy lights, blooming flowers, and fragrant herbs. A grand entrance awaits the guests, with a cascading floral archway leading to the ceremony site, where rows of hay bales covered in lace provide seating. The bride, wearing a stunning lace gown and a flower crown, walks down an aisle lined with wildflowers, while the groom awaits her under a beautifully decorated arbor made of reclaimed wood.

The ceremony is intimate and heartfelt, with the sounds of birds chirping and the gentle breeze rustling through the trees creating an enchanting atmosphere. After exchanging vows, the newlyweds lead their guests to a lavish outdoor reception area, complete with long wooden tables adorned with elegant centerpieces of wildflowers, flickering candles, and crystal chandeliers hanging from tree branches. A live band sets the tone for the evening, playing country tunes and filling the air with joyous melodies.

Mouth-watering dishes made with locally sourced ingredients are served, showcasing the region's culinary delights. As the sun sets, guests gather around a cozy bonfire, sharing stories and toasting marshmallows. The evening ends with a spectacular fireworks display, lighting up the starry sky and leaving everyone in awe. An elaborate country wedding is a celebration that embraces the beauty of nature, creating memories that will last a lifetime.

Jake worried excessively about the plan, questioning Roz about who would cover the lavish expenses. Roz assured him that her mother and father were taking care of most of the arrangements, so he was not about to worry. She had been looking forward to this since she was a small child, and Jake Sutton would not spoil it for her.

Roz did an internship at Grady Memorial in downtown Atlanta, a huge medical facility that treated hundreds of patients per day. She attended classes in the morning at South University and drove downtown to Grady to work an eight-hour shift. It was very stressful, but Roz was determined. She saved her money towards her wedding but never shared that with Jake.

While plans were being made for the "Wedding of the Century" (as they called it), all team members busied themselves with schoolwork. Jake promised Roz not to take any more trips on his own with his friends. He agreed, and all was well. Mia was continuing to carry on without Brian, but it was very difficult. She had found another classmate at UGA who was also working on the Uganda Project, and they were living together.

In December 1980, just a few months before Jake's wedding, he received devastating news about his mother's health. Jake's mom had recently visited her doctor for a routine check-up, during which the doctor discovered concerning lumps in both of her breasts. It had been over two years since her last mammogram, and she had noticed no abnormalities during self-examinations.

Concerned about the potential severity of the situation, they promptly scheduled a biopsy to determine the nature of the lumps. Unfortunately, the results confirmed their worst fears - the lumps were cancerous. The medical professionals informed Jake and his family that the cancer cells were spreading rapidly throughout his mother's body.

Roz told Jake that she had a couple of papers to write and would come down to Atlanta as soon as she was able. Jake immediately went home for Christmas break after clearing it with his professors. He had to be with his mother. She was his rock. His father had been his guide for most of his life, but his mother was there for every football, soccer, and baseball game since little league. She stood by him through everything. He would not desert her now at this trying time in her life. She just had to get well, he thought.

The hospital scheduled the double mastectomy within days, and Jake, his father, younger sister Amber, and Roz were there to support her and await the surgeon's report.

Within a couple of hours, the surgeon came out of the operating room and said that he had successfully retrieved all the lumps during the surgical procedure. However, his tone and demeanor were far from encouraging as he delivered the news that the cancer was still present. The atmosphere in the waiting room grew heavy with despair as the surgeon explained to the anxious family that their loved one's prognosis was uncertain. He informed them that administering chemotherapy could extend her life for two months to a year. However, he also emphasized the gravity of the situation by mentioning that, without the chemotherapy, the outlook was bleak. The family was now faced with a tough decision that carried immense consequences for their loved one's future. Jake spoke up, saying his mom was tough and would remain hopeful.

Upon regaining consciousness in her hospital room, Mrs. Sutton observed those gathered around her. Mr. Sutton, sitting on her bedside, took her hand and told her that the doctor had removed all the lumps, but there was still the presence of cancer and chemotherapy would hopefully resolve that. Mrs. Sutton asked how long the chemo would take and Roz then told her a couple of months to a year. Mr. Sutton informed his wife that the prognosis was not good and broke down into tears. Everyone surrounded the bed and commiserated together.

Mrs. Sutton then spoke (adamantly): "I still have a wedding to plan for next May. I will NOT allow the doctor, nor any chemotherapy, to take that away from me!"

Atlanta Journal Headlines, February 8, 1981:

Unusually Heavy Snowfall Blankets Atlanta in

Early February

In a surprising turn of events, Atlanta, known for its mild winters, experienced an unprecedented snowfall in early February. A thick layer of snow covered the city and surrounding areas, turning the typically temperate region into a winter wonderland. The snowfall was not just a mere dusting, but a substantial accumulation, reaching depths of approximately 6 inches. This unexpected weather phenomenon brought about a host of challenges and delighted residents who could enjoy rare winter activities such as sledding and building snowmen.

The snowfall began in the early hours of the morning, catching many Atlantans off guard. The sudden change in weather prompted a flurry of activity as schools and businesses scrambled to respond. City workers dispatched road crews to clear major thoroughfares; meanwhile, citizens eagerly dug out their winter gear from their closets.

The heavy snowfall had a significant impact on transportation and infrastructure throughout the Atlanta area. Major highways and roads quickly became treacherous, with icy patches and reduced visibility, causing many accidents and delays. Public transportation services were also heavily affected, as buses and trains faced difficulties navigating the snowy terrain. Cancelations and delays of flights in and out of Hartsfield-Jackson Atlanta International

Airport frustrated travelers.

Despite the challenges, the unexpected snowfall also brought a sense of excitement and joy to the city's residents. Families took advantage of the rare opportunity to engage in traditional winter activities, with children eagerly building snow forts and engaging in friendly snowball fights. The laughter and sounds of sleds filled the air as parks and open spaces became bustling playgrounds.

As the snow gradually melted in the following days, life in Atlanta returned to its usual rhythm. However, the memories of this extraordinary snowfall will linger, reminding residents that even in a region known for its mild winters, nature can still surprise and enchant.

Another winter soon developed in the Sutton family. As the chilly winds blew and the snowflakes fell, Mrs. Sutton's health condition took a turn for the worse. Because she was concerned about her deteriorating health, she sought medical attention; the hospital then admitted her for further evaluation. The doctors conducted various tests to determine the underlying cause of her declining health and administered fluids to replenish her body. It was a challenging time for the Sutton family as they anxiously awaited the results and hoped for a positive outcome.

Mr. Sutton, Jake, Roz, and Amy went down to Rig-

gers Funeral Home two days later to make plans for Mrs.
Sutton's funeral. The winter had been harsh, with bitter
cold temperatures and heavy snowfall, posing yet another
challenge for Jake and his family during an already difficult
time. As they grieved the passing of Mrs. Sutton, Roz,
a close family friend, emerged as a sturdy figure in their
lives. With her unwavering support, encouragement, and
endless hope, Roz became a pillar of strength for the Sutton family. She was always there, ready to lend a listening
ear, offer comforting words, and provide solace during
this trying ordeal. Roz's devout faith was clear, as she frequently prayed with the family, helping them find peace
and comfort in their darkest moments. Her presence and
unwavering support were invaluable to the Suttons as they
navigated through the painful process of saying goodbye
to their beloved Mrs. Sutton. Sarah and Mia came for the
funeral service and helped console the family.

Mia shared a charming townhouse in the heart of
Athens with Sara Thompson. The townhouse, boast-
ing two spacious bedrooms, provided more than enough
room for the enthusiastic duo. As they eagerly expected
their upcoming mission trip, they meticulously coordi-
nated with the Uganda Project, a renowned organization
dedicated to making a positive impact in underprivileged
communities. With June just around the corner, Sarah and

Mia couldn't contain their excitement as they prepared to embark on their journey. In Mia's mind, Brian was going to Uganda with her and Sarah, even if only spiritually.

Graduation day finally arrived, marking a significant milestone in both of their lives and serving as a poignant reminder of the incredible adventure that lay ahead. Sarah was from the small town of Leesburg, Georgia, just outside of Albany. She had always wanted to be involved in world hunger since her childhood. Sarah Thompson was a beautiful and petite young lady with a penchant for peanut brittle. She hailed from a peanut growing part of Georgia. In fact, her father was a peanut farmer, so peanut brittle was a staple around their home and her father made the best of anyone, giving it away to anyone who desired it. Mia had taken a liking to the brittle and could not pass up its crunch and sweetness.

Sadness gripped Mia often after Brian's tragic death. All she could see in her mind's eye was Brian lying there on a stormy mountainside, during a heavy thunderstorm, beneath an ancient oak tree that pinned him to the earth. The image haunted her, replaying repeatedly like a painful movie scene that refused to fade away. It was a cold and dreary night when the unexpected tragedy unfolded; the rain pouring down relentlessly, adding an eerie backdrop to the darkness that enveloped the mountains. Brian's sudden death sent shockwaves through Mia's entire being, shattering her sense of security and leaving her feeling utterly helpless. The loss was profound, and the weight of grief bore down on her like an unbearable burden. Tragedy had reared its ugly head that fateful night, tearing apart the fabric of Mia's world and forever changing the course of her life.

Could it have been the many omens the team received throughout their trip? From the sudden thunderstorm at Gooch Gap that delayed their departure, to the broken compass that led them astray, and the eerie howling of winds that echoed through the night, the signs were hard to ignore. What were those signs trying to tell the campers? Should they have gone to the beach instead of the mountains? Would things have been different if they had chosen another path?

These questions plagued their minds as they struggled to make sense of the series of unfortunate events. Is life not that way? Mia, with a furrowed brow, wondered why bad things happen to good people. Is anything for certain in this life? The uncertainty of their situation only deepened as they realized that sometimes, no matter how carefully we plan or how good our intentions, life has a way of throwing curveballs we can never fully comprehend.

During their four years at Young Harris, Brian and Mia's

paths crossed for three years, and they enjoyed a good life. Mia knew unconditional love for the first time in her life and dearly loved Brian for everything he stood for. Without him, she must continue piecing together a future that would please Brian.

Mia would forever remember Brian's face beneath that gigantic oak tree. It was a bittersweet moment as Brian whispered his last words to her before his passing. With a tender voice, he mustered the strength to said, "Mia, I ... love ... you." Those words, filled with pure affection, would forever resonate within her heart. The love they shared was a precious gift that would accompany her throughout the journey of her life. It would not overpower her future, but serve as a steadfast presence, a constant companion that would bring her solace and strength during both joyful and challenging times.

Mia remembered Brian's life hanging in the balance as he teetered on the edge of a cliff at the treacherous Black Mountain. In a heart-stopping turn of events, he narrowly escaped a fatal fall, thanks to the heroic efforts of his dedicated team. However, the celebration that followed was premature, as the danger had not completely subsided. Among the team members, Jake emerged as the luckiest soul, as he fearlessly risked his own life to rescue his best friend from the ledge below. In a moment, fueled by adrenaline and unwavering bravery, Jake descended the perilous slope, defying the potential of his own sudden demise.

As the team basked in the relief of Brian's successful rescue, the true extent of the danger they had faced sank in. Black Mountain, with its jagged cliffs and treacherous terrain, had claimed a few lives in the past. Brian's brush with death served as a stark reminder of the unforgiving nature of this formidable peak. The celebratory atmosphere quickly shifted to one of introspection and gratitude.

Of all the team members, Jake stood out as the embodiment of sheer luck and incredible bravery. His swift actions and unwavering determination had saved Brian from a potentially tragic fate. In the critical moments following Brian's fall, Jake's instincts kicked in, overriding any fear or hesitation. Without a second thought, he navigated the treacherous path down the cliff, defying gravity and the looming threat of his own demise.

The adrenaline coursing through Jake's veins propelled him forward, each step an audacious act of defiance against the perils of Black Mountain. As he descended, the sheer magnitude of the cliff became apparent, with its unforgiving rocks and sheer drops. The sense of urgency and the knowledge that every passing second could make the difference between life and death only fueled Jake's determination.

With each careful maneuver, Jake inched closer to Brian, his focus unwavering despite the precariousness of his own situation. The sound of his pounding heart and the rush of wind against his face broke the deafening silence only. Every muscle in his body strained as he fought against gravity, determined to reach his best friend and pull him back from the brink of disaster.

Finally, after what felt like an eternity, Jake reached Brian's side. The overwhelming relief that washed over him was palpable as he clasped Brian's trembling hand. Their faithful team members above and two passing backpackers would pull them to safety. The team's combined strength and determination pushed them forward. The team watched in awe and disbelief as Brian and Jake emerged from the abyss, their bond stronger than ever, forged in the crucible of near tragedy.

Brian's miraculous escape from the clutches of death at Black Mountain served as a poignant reminder of the fragility of life and the unbreakable bonds that exist between loyal friends. Jake's selfless bravery and unwavering determination will forever remain in their memories, a testament to courage and the triumph of the human spirit. As Mia reflected on the events that unfolded on that fateful day, she was reminded of the unpredictable nature of life, urging her to cherish every moment and to never underestimate the indomitable strength that lies within each of us.

17

Roger and Mia's Adventures

Roger and Mia's marriage blossomed beyond Mia's expectations. Roger, an enthusiastic plant lover and nature enthusiast, suggested a honeymoon destination that perfectly aligned with his passions. He proposed a trip to the picturesque town of Helen, Georgia, known for its stunning natural landscapes and charming atmosphere. Nestled in the Blue Ridge Mountains, Helen offered a unique blend of outdoor adventure and romantic ambiance, making it an ideal choice for the couple's post-wedding getaway. Surrounded by breathtaking scenery, including cascading waterfalls, dense forests, and meandering rivers, Roger and Mia could immerse themselves in the beauty of nature while enjoying each other's company. Helen owned a vibrant botanical garden where Roger could fully indulge his and Mia's love for plants.

Hiking, biking, river tubing, and horseback riding were among the many activities this quaint town offered, ensuring the couple's honeymoon would be filled with unforgettable experiences. With Roger's thoughtful suggestion, Mia eagerly expected their honeymoon in Helen, Georgia, excited about the adventures and cherished memories that awaited them amidst the natural wonders of this enchanting destination.

Their drive from Athens to Helen took them through many little, small mountain towns and villages, many of them nestled in the mountain coves. The picturesque scenery was breathtaking, with lush green valleys, towering peaks, and cascading waterfalls. As they wound their way along the winding mountain roads, the charm and tranquility of the small communities captivated them. Each town had its own unique character, with quaint houses and vibrant local businesses lining the streets. The locals greeted them with warm smiles and friendly waves, making them feel instantly welcome.

They stopped at a few of the towns along the way, exploring the local shops and indulging in delicious homemade treats at cozy cafes. The drive itself was an adventure, as they navigated steep inclines and hairpin turns, but the stunning views made every twist and turn worthwhile. They couldn't help but marvel at the natural beauty that

surrounded them, feeling a deep sense of peace and serenity. This drive through the small mountain towns and
villages truly created a memorable journey, highlighting
hidden gems off the beaten path.

Mia constantly remembered the terrible ordeal she'd experienced near Helen. It haunted her thoughts, a constant
presence that she couldn't escape. The memory of that
fateful night weighed heavily on her, its grip on her psy-
che growing stronger with each passing day. Mia prayed
fervently, her heart pleading that Roger, her beloved husband, wouldn't take that ill-fated trip over to Highway 129
and to the Walasi-Yi Center. The thought of him venturing into that area, so close to where she had faced unimaginable horror, sent shivers down her spine. It was like fear
itself had wrapped its icy fingers around her mind, refusing
to let go. Mia's anxiety intensified as the day approached,
her instincts screaming at her to protect the man she loved
from the darkness that lurked in that place.

Isn't it amazing how our worst fears come at a time of
joy? It's as if life has a way of throwing us curveballs just
when we least expect them. Take, for example, the story
of Emma, a young woman who had just received a promotion at work and was on cloud nine. She had worked
tirelessly for years, sacrificing time with loved ones and
countless hours of sleep to climb the corporate ladder.

Finally, she received the deserved recognition and promotion as a reward for her hard work. As she celebrated her success with friends and family, little did she know that her worst fear was about to become a reality. Amid her joy, she received a phone call informing her that her father had been involved in a serious car accident. Suddenly, the world came crashing down around her, and her elation turned to despair. It seemed almost cruel that just when she was experiencing a well-deserved moment of happiness, life had tested her resilience and strength. This scenario is common. It is often during our moments of triumph and bliss that our worst fears come knocking at our door. It is as if the universe wants to remind us that life is full of uncertainties, and even in our happiest moments, we must remain prepared to face whatever challenges may come our way. So, the next time you find yourself in a moment of pure joy, embrace it fully, but also be mindful that life is unpredictable, and our worst fears may lurk just around the corner.

The two checked into a Best Western motel near the Chattahoochee River. It was very scenic, and the town of Helen was only a short walk across the river bridge. That night, the two feasted on beer brats and champagne, two unimaginable combinations! Roger made a toast to the two of them and promised to always love her and protect her. A yodeling group entertained them after the meal and they thoroughly enjoyed the dancing.

Helen, a charming town nestled in the heart of Georgia, is reminiscent of a picturesque village in Switzerland. Its downtown area boasts an enchanting collection of buildings, each meticulously designed in the Swiss style. These architectural gems exude a captivating allure, with their intricate details and eye-catching facades. Strolling through Helen's streets transports visitors to a world mirroring the beauty and charm of the Swiss countryside. The town's commitment to preserving its unique identity is clear in the careful craftsmanship and attention to detail highlighted in every building. From cozy alpine chalets to grand clock towers, the diverse array of structures truly captures the essence of Swiss architecture. Helen's downtown area is a testament to the town's commitment to providing an immersive experience for residents and tourists alike, where every corner reveals a new delight for the senses.

After an early dinner at a charming local restaurant, the two newlyweds, Roger and Mia, took a leisurely stroll down to the banks of the Chattahoochee River. The sun was setting, casting a warm golden glow on the surroundings. As they walked hand in hand, they couldn't help but marvel at the breathtaking view of the river, its swirling ripples cascading down the hill from the majestic Mountains in the distance.

Spring had arrived in full force, painting the landscape in vibrant colors. Lilies, daffodils, and trilliums adorned the riverbank, creating a picturesque scene that seemed straight out of a fairytale. Blooming flowers filled the air with their sweet scent, enhancing the moment's enchanting ambiance.

However, as they stood by the river, Roger noticed a slight hint of unease in Mia's eyes. Concerned for his beloved wife, he gently broached the subject. Sensing that something was bothering her, he asked, "Mia, my dear, what's going on? You haven't seemed like yourself since we arrived. It's like you fear that something is going to happen."

Mia hesitated for a moment before responding, her voice filled with a mixture of vulnerability and apprehension. "Ah, it's not really anything important, Roger. These mountains have a way of drawing you back into their mystique if you're not careful."

Roger, being the understanding partner he was, had a deep understanding of Mia's past. He knew about Brian, Mia's first love, and his sudden death in these very mountains. Although they had discussed it before, Roger couldn't help but wonder if Mia's unease stemmed from those painful memories.

"Honey, you know I understand what happened with you and the team," Roger reassured her, his voice filled with sincerity. "I'll not even mention it again if that's what's troubling you." Mia felt a surge of gratitude for her caring husband, who always knew how to provide comfort and support when she needed it most.

Together, they stood by the river, the soothing sound of flowing water creating a sense of calmness around them. As the sun dipped below the horizon, casting a beautiful array of colors across the sky, Roger wrapped his arms around Mia, holding her tight. In that moment, they both knew that no matter what challenges lay ahead, they would face them together, their love stronger than ever amidst the allure of the mountains.

After a restful night's sleep at the Best Western, Mia and Roger woke up feeling refreshed and ready to explore. They took a leisurely stroll through the quaint streets, taking in the charming sights and sounds of the village. As they wandered further down the road, they stumbled upon a unique shop that caught their attention. The sign above the entrance read "Betty's Grocery," a name that had a certain charm to it. Intrigued, they stepped inside to discover a world of treasures.

Betty's Grocery had been a beloved establishment in the

community for years, serving as a haven for backpackers and campers who ventured off the beaten trail and hiked down the highway from Unicoi Gap. The shop catered to these adventurous souls, providing all kinds of supplies they might need for their outdoor expeditions. From sturdy backpacks and durable camping gear to essential food supplies, Betty's had it all.

But that wasn't all. Mia and Roger soon realized that Betty's was not just your ordinary grocery store. As they explored further, they discovered an array of goods that went beyond the typical camping supplies. A wine store nestled in the corner offered a selection of fine wines from local vineyards, tempting them with the prospect of a relaxing evening after a long day of hiking.

The surprises didn't end there. Betty's also featured handcrafted gifts from local artisans. Mia's eyes sparkled with delight as she admired the intricate pottery, beautiful jewelry, and unique wooden carvings on display. It was the perfect place to find a special souvenir to remember their visit.

After their morning stroll, Mia and Roger smelled a delightful aroma from Betty's Grocery and it caught their attention. Curiosity piqued, they followed the delicious scent and found themselves inside a small diner nestled within the shop. The cozy atmosphere and friendly staff welcomed them, and they treated themselves to a hot breakfast.

The food served at the diner exceeded their expectations. From fluffy pancakes drizzled with maple syrup to sizzling bacon and eggs cooked to perfection, every bite was a delight to their taste buds. Mia and Roger couldn't help but savor the flavors, feeling grateful for stumbling upon this hidden gem.

Their visit to Betty's Grocery turned out to be a delightful surprise, offering not just a place to stock up on essentials but also a charming experience filled with unexpected discoveries. With their bellies full and a newfound appreciation for the village, Mia and Roger continued their exploration, eager to see what other treasures awaited them in this enchanting corner of the world.

At the Presbyterian Church along the highway near Betty's, Mia and her husband Roger stood in awe as they observed the bustling scene unfolding before them. Several adventurous backpackers arrived in their vehicles, filling the church parking lot with excitement on a beautiful summer morning. The air was thick with anticipation as these intrepid explorers stepped out of their cars and meticulously fastened their backpacks, preparing themselves for the journey that lay ahead. Mia couldn't help but feel a mix of emotions stirring within her. On one hand, she felt a pang of envy, wishing she could be among them, embarking on an unforgettable adventure. However, a tinge of fear intertwined with her envy. She knew all too well the challenges that awaited these hikers on the trail up to Unicoi Gap. The rugged terrain, unpredictable weather, and physical demands of the hike were not to be taken lightly. Mia couldn't help but feel a sense of trepidation as she watched these brave souls set off, their determination shining through their eyes. Deep down, she wondered if she had the strength and resilience to face her fears.

Does one ever truly forget the tragedies of life? This is a question that many have pondered throughout history. Tragedies, whether personal or collective, have a profound impact on our lives and shape our perspective. While time may lessen the intensity of emotions associated with these events, the memories and scars remain. The pain and sorrow experienced during a tragedy become etched into our consciousness, serving as a constant reminder of the fragility and unpredictability of life. Tragedies affect not only individuals; their impact resonates with families, communities, and nations. Generations pass down the collective memory of a tragedy, ensuring that its lessons are not forgotten. Although individuals may cope and move forward, the tragedies of life leave an indelible mark that lingers in the depths of our minds.

Mia, a resilient and determined woman, was determined to overcome the one glaring tragedy that had cast a shadow over her life. Through her teaching career and her loving marriage to Roger, a compassionate and supportive man, Mia found solace and strength. As they embarked on a trip to Helen, a charming town known for its picturesque beauty, Mia hoped that the serene surroundings would provide her with a much-needed sense of healing and peace. However, their visit to Helen ended the following day, and Mia and Roger began their drive back home to Athens, their hearts filled with memories and their spirits uplifted by the love and connection they had experienced during their trip.

18

Mia's Reflections

Mia called Roz on Monday night, following their exciting trip to Helen. The moment Roz answered the call, she couldn't wait to share the news with Mia - she was expecting twins! The joy in Roz's voice was contagious as she revealed the twins were due to arrive the following February. Overwhelmed with happiness, Roz and her husband Jake had already chosen Mia as the Godmother for their precious little ones. This news solidified the deep bond between the two friends, as Mia felt honored to take on such a significant role in the lives of these soon-to-be-born twins.

Roz and Jake had bought a ten-acre farm near the Red Barn venue where they had married north of Roswell, Georgia, and had a few goats and cattle. Jake and his father's crew had built the home in a grand old Victorian style (Roz's wish). Jake and his father's crew built it with all the inside and outside ornamentation that screamed

Victorian.

Their conversation lasted a good while since it had been a year since Mia and Roger's wedding. Mia eagerly shared with Roz the details of her recent trip to Helen. She recounted the whirlwind of emotions she experienced while there, as it was in that very location where her past relationship with Brian had blossomed and crumbled. Mia vividly described the sight of backpackers emerging from their cars and embarking on the road to Unicoi Gap. As she reminisced, Roz listened attentively, offering her perspective on the matter. "Mia," she gently interjected, "we can't allow ourselves to dwell on these memories endlessly. They can become like cancerous thoughts that erode our minds and hinder our ability to find true happiness."

The two promised to meet somewhere between Roswell and Athens in the weeks to come and talk about everything that has transpired in their lives. She told Mia that Jake was working at his father's engineering firm and doing well, already making over the $100,000 thousand dollar mark! Not only was he excelling in his career, but he also seemed to have found his passion for engineering. Roz had pursued her dreams of becoming a nurse and was now teaching nursing at South University, the very school where she had graduated with her master's in nursing. Her dedication and expertise had earned her a respectable salary. Together, they were a power couple, financially stable and ready to take on whatever challenges life threw their way. However, Roz acknowledged they couldn't ignore the unpredictable nature of the future. They understood unforeseen circumstances could arise, but dwelling on them would only lead to losing their sanity. With a positive outlook and a firm foundation, they were determined to face whatever consequences may come their way.

Mia discovered Roz was involved in a secret project that she had been working on for months. It was a groundbreaking innovation in artificial intelligence, a project that had the potential to revolutionize the industry. Roz's explanation of the details amazed Mia with its complexity and ingenuity. The project involved developing a highly advanced neural network that could mimic human behavior and emotions with astonishing accuracy. It was designed to learn and adapt, constantly evolving to become more human-like. Roz had been dedicating countless hours to perfecting the algorithms and training the network, pouring her heart and soul into this ambitious endeavor. Mia couldn't help but feel a mix of awe and curiosity as she listened to Roz's animated explanation. She realized her friend had been keeping this incredible secret hidden from the world, and now she was privileged to be let in on it. Mia knew that this project had the potential to change everything, and she couldn't wait to see how it would unfold.

Roz suggested that the four of them, Jake, Roz, Roger, and Mia, take a cruise together after the babies are born and around a year old, and Mia agreed it would be great. Mia was not sure that she would still fit into Roz's life. Over a year had passed since they'd last seen each other, and Roz's life was completely different.

Mia's life had also changed since she began her teaching career at UGA. She had helped develop several new hybrids of plants that had earned her significant acclaim but had left the classroom for the research lab to do so. She loved the teaching aspect, but the University saw her abilities to do hands-on horticulture and offered her a marvelous job, so she took it with Roger's insistence.

Paths cross in life, sometimes by chance and sometimes by design. People from different walks of life come together, their journeys intersecting and intertwining. These encounters can occur in various settings, such as at work, in school, or during social events. Whether it is a brief encounter or a long-lasting connection, these moments have the potential to shape our lives in unexpected ways. They provide opportunities for growth, learning, and new perspectives.

When paths cross, we have the chance to connect with

others, share experiences, and create meaningful relationships. These interactions can lead to collaboration, support, and even lifelong friendships. As we navigate through life, it is important to embrace these encounters and the potential they hold, for they can enrich our lives in ways we may have never imagined.

Years ago, on the Appalachian Trail, four young adults formed a close-knit group, like family or best friends. Together, they would face the unknown and cast caution to the wind. It was their time in the sun; adventure lay ahead of them. Roz, Jake, Brian, and Mia took the trip of a lifetime, not knowing fully the mysteries of every turn along that trip.

They had meticulously planned their journey, ensuring they had all the gear and supplies to sustain them through the grueling terrain and unpredictable weather. They filled their backpacks with lightweight tents, sleeping bags, cooking utensils, and enough food for weeks. Having studied countless stories and maps from previous hikers on the same trail, they were still unprepared for the breathtaking beauty and challenges that awaited.

With hearts full of excitement and anticipation, they set foot on the trail, ready to conquer whatever obstacles lay in their path. Little did they know that this adventure would not only test their physical strength and endurance, but also their bonds of friendship and resilience. As they ventured deeper into the wilderness, they encountered steep ascents that left their legs trembling and treacherous descents that required utmost concentration.

The dense forests enveloped them, and the sweet scent of pine filled their lungs. They witnessed majestic waterfalls cascading down rocky cliffs, and the serenity of untouched lakes reflecting the vibrant colors of the surrounding foliage. Each passing day brought new challenges and moments of awe-inspiring beauty.

They faced thunderstorms that soaked them to the bone, yet their spirits remained undeterred. They navigated through narrow paths that seemed to disappear into thin air, relying on their intuition and trust in each other. Huddled together around a campfire, they spent their nights sharing stories, laughter, and dreams under the star-studded sky. Reveling in the simplicity of life on the trail, they disconnected from the noise of civilization and became fully immersed in the rawness of nature.

Along the way, they encountered fellow hikers, forming temporary alliances and exchanging tales of their respective journeys. They learned to appreciate the kindness of strangers who offered them encouragement and shared valuable tips. As they neared the end of their expedition, they couldn't help but feel a mix of pride and nostalgia.

They would forever cherish the memories they created, the obstacles they overcame, and the unbreakable bonds they forged.

The Appalachian Trail had tested their limits, pushed them to their boundaries, and rewarded them with a sense of accomplishment and a newfound appreciation for the beauty of the natural world. This epic adventure had transformed them individually and as a group, solidifying their friendship and leaving them with a hunger for more extraordinary experiences. As they reached the last stretch of the trail, they knew their lives would never be the same. The Appalachian Trail had become a part of their story, a testament to their resilience, and a reminder that sometimes, the greatest adventures lie just beyond the next turn.

And then the tragedy with Brian and his untimely passing would forever engrave itself indelibly in their hearts and minds. The night of horrors, Mia would forever call it, changed her life completely! Her fiancé, the love of her life, had died from the falling tree during the worst thunderstorm of her existence. The shock and grief of losing him so suddenly and tragically rocked Mia's world, leaving her feeling numb and lost. A blur of funeral preparations and tearful goodbyes ensued in the following days, as friends and family gathered to mourn Brian's untimely passing.

The weight of grief was heavy, but Mia found solace in the support of loved ones and the shared memories of a man who had brought joy and love into her life.

Graduation, which should have been a time of celebration, became bittersweet as Mia gave her valedictory speech and walked across the stage without the presence of her beloved Brian. Every milestone, every achievement, was now tinged with the absence of the person who had been her biggest cheerleader.

Determined to honor Brian's memory and find purpose in her pain, Mia embarked on a journey that would take her to Uganda. It was there, amidst the backdrop of a foreign land and a different culture, that Mia found healing and a renewed sense of purpose. The experience of volunteering and helping others in need allowed her to channel her grief into something positive, creating a legacy for Brian that would live on in the lives she touched. Each moment in Uganda became a testament to the resilience of the human spirit and the power of love to overcome even the darkest of times.

As Mia reflected on the journey she had taken since that fateful night, she realized that while the pain of losing Brian would never fully go away, she had grown stronger and learned to carry his memory with her in a way that brought light into her life. The tragedy had forever changed her and the team, but it had also shaped her into a woman of strength, compassion, and resilience. The memories created during those challenging times would remain etched in her heart, serving as a constant reminder of the love she had lost and the love she had gained through the journey of healing and self-discovery.

19

The Endless Trail

Embarking on the Appalachian Trail (A.T.) is more than just a physical journey across 2,200 miles of rugged terrain; it's a metaphor for life's continuous journey. As hikers set foot on the A.T., they begin a transformative adventure that challenges their strength, endurance, and spirit. But what happens when they reach the trail's end? Does the journey truly conclude, or does it simply transition into a new phase? There is the idea that no trail ever truly ends; instead, each trail is intertwined with the next, forming an unending path of growth and discovery.

The start of the A.T. is marked by anticipation and excitement. For many, it represents a break from the routines of daily life and a chance to reconnect with nature. As hikers navigate the diverse landscapes of mountains, valleys, and forests, they encounter physical and mental challenges that test their limits. Along the way, they forge bonds with fellow hikers, experience moments of solitude, and gain a deeper appreciation for the natural world. Yet, beyond the physical accomplishments, there is an internal journey taking place—a journey of self-discovery and personal growth.

Standing at the final summit of the A.T., hikers often expect a sense of closure, a culmination of their efforts and perseverance. The view from the top is breathtaking, a testament to their hard work and determination. However, seasoned adventurers know that this sense of completion is fleeting. The end of the A.T. is not a definitive conclusion but a transition point. It's a moment to reflect on the journey, celebrate the achievements, and acknowledge the lessons learned. More importantly, it's a door opening to new possibilities and adventures.

Life is a series of connected trails, each leading to the next. Completing the A.T. is not the end of one's journey but a steppingstone to new beginnings. The experiences gained on the trail—resilience, perseverance, and an appreciation for simplicity—become tools for navigating future challenges. Every trail hiked, whether in the wilderness or in life, contributes to the continuous path of personal growth. Just as the seasons change, so do the trails we follow, each one offering new opportunities for learning and exploration.

Returning from the A.T., hikers often find that they are not the same person who set out on the trail. The journey has transformed them, providing new perspectives and insights. This personal growth is not confined to the trail; it extends into everyday life. The end of the A.T. is a new starting point, inspiring hikers to seek out new adventures, set new goals, and continue their journey of self-discovery. The lessons learned on the trail—patience, determination, and the value of persistence—become guiding principles for future endeavors.

In the words of John Muir, "The mountains are calling, and I must go." This sentiment captures the essence of the endless trail. The end of the Appalachian Trail is not a conclusion but an invitation to continue exploring, dreaming, and venturing into the unknown. Trails intersect, diverge, and reconnect, much like the paths of our lives. Each journey, whether on the A.T. or beyond, is a chapter in the never-ending story of adventure and growth. So, does a trail ever end? Perhaps not. Instead, it evolves with us, becoming an integral part of our lifelong journey.

Epilogue

The trip from Dahlonega up Highway 60 to Woody Gap was an exhilarating experience for Brian and Zachary, ten-year-old twins. Their parents, Jake and Roz Sutton, who were equally excited about the adventure, accompanied them. As the family reached Woody Gap, Jake pulled off the highway and took a moment to share a few intriguing stories from the past. Brian and Zachary's curiosity arose instantly, and they eagerly listened to their father. With their young minds full of questions and a thirst for knowledge, the twins were ready to explore and learn more about the history and wonders that awaited them at Woody Gap.

Thirteen years had passed when Jake, Roz, Brian, and Mia stopped at this crossing following their ordeal with Brian up on Black Mountain. Yet, to Jake, it seemed like yesterday. He will forever remember that moment vividly. It was a crisp spring day; the air filled with the scent of fallen leaves and the promise of a new beginning. The group had embarked on a hiking adventure that twisted into a harrowing experience. They had ventured up Black Mountain, a treacherous peak that held secrets and dangers unknown to them.

As they descended the mountain, their legs weary and their spirits dampened, they stumbled upon Gooch's Grocery Store. The quaint little shop stood as an oasis amid their tumultuous journeys. Its weathered wooden exterior and creaky screen door welcomed them with open arms. Inside, a delightful old couple, Mr. and Mrs. Gooch, who possessed an otherworldly wisdom, greeted them. Their warm smiles and genuine concern for the weary travelers instantly put them at ease.

While resting at the store, a peculiar creature caught Jake's eye—the Flying Possum. A shelf held the flying possum, its wings spread wide in a frozen moment of flight. Its presence added an air of enchantment to the already magical atmosphere. And just when Jake thought he had seen it all, he noticed a peculiar creature called the Jack-a-Lope. It was a mythical hybrid of a jackrabbit and an antelope, mounted on the wall as a trophy. Its wide, glassy eyes followed Jake's every move, as if it held some secret message.

But amidst the charm and wonder of the store, there was a sense of urgency. During their mountain ordeal, their dear friend Brian suffered an injury. His face etched with pain, he sat in a worn-out chair, his body exhausted from the physical and emotional toll. Concerned for his well-being, Jake and the others took a much-needed respite at the store. They knew Brian needed time to heal, both physically and mentally, before continuing their journey.

As they sat together, sharing stories and laughter, the group found solace in their temporary sanctuary. The old couple's kindness, the mysterious creatures, and the camaraderie amongst friends created a sense of hope amidst the uncertainty. Little did they know that this fateful encounter at Gooch's Grocery Store would forever shape their lives and bond them together in ways they could never have imagined.

Roz shared a few tidbits with the boys, delighting them while Jake drove down the curvy, steeply descending road, arriving at Gooch's Grocery in the valley below. Time seemed to have changed everything. Someone had boarded up and closed the old store, posting a FOR SALE sign out front. The stacks of wood were still under the shelter, but the store was empty! Jake had so hoped his boys could meet the old couple, but he would later learn at a convenience store down the road that the couple had died a few years before. It broke Roz's and Jake's hearts to hear the news.

Jake, a seasoned adventurer, embarked on a journey up

Highway 60, eventually arriving back at Gooch's store. With a sense of familiarity, he made a right turn, leading him onto Gooch Gap Road. This road would soon guide him through a captivating landscape, winding its way through a maze of charming houses, a bustling chicken farm, and even a flourishing fish farm. As the gravel road stretched out ahead, Jake's anticipation grew, knowing that it would lead him and his beloved wife, Roz, to a place that held a special significance in their hearts—Gooch Gap. This picturesque spot had witnessed unforgettable moments in their lives, including the unforgettable "Storm of the Century" that they had experienced together as a team.

Pulling the car off the road, Jake and Roz then took the children up the winding trail south to Gooch Gap Shelter. Upon arrival, they found the place unchanged from their previous visit years earlier. The twins were excited. They wanted to know everything about the place, so Jake and Roz shared their experiences. Their eyes wide, the twins hung on their parents' every word as they received a history lesson about the A.T., Gooch Gap, and the terrible night of the storm. All four of them sat on the edge of the shelter and talked for a long while.

And then they just listened. The boys, Brian and Zachary, were quiet and expectant. Their dad, a seasoned hiker and nature enthusiast, had suddenly stopped talking and said, "Did you hear that?" The boys, their curiosity piqued, strained their ears but could not discern any distinct sound. "There it is again. Did you hear it?" Their dad persisted.

Brian, the older of the two, shook his head and replied, "No, daddy, I only hear the gentle rustling of leaves and the soft whisper of wind in the trees." It seemed as if no one heard the voices except Jake.

Today, somewhere along this wild, exciting, and treacherous path, someone hears the enigmatic sounds and relays the voices heard, whispering in the wind, which hold the secrets of the untamed wilderness.